"I see y
Devlin sai

Hilary turned around to look at her regular parking spot. Devlin was in the way. A tiny voice inside her told her to stop staring. She could, she thought, if he stopped staring at her first. But those blue-green eyes held her mesmerized. She could feel her body respond, and she could see his awareness of her reaction in his quickened breathing.

He reached across the space between them until his fingers touched her hair. They threaded through the strands slowly, as if testing them against his skin.

"Do you know you never wear it free like this?" he said in a quiet voice.

"Yes, I do," she said, surprised her calm tone betrayed none of the wild confusion bursting inside her.

"I've never seen it," he answered softly.

"I should go," she said. But she didn't move.

"Yes, you should," he said, even as his hand cupped her cheek.

The space between them suddenly closed to nothing. Their mouths met instantly, hungrily, in a thorough, breath-stealing kiss that inflamed her. His arm came around her, pulling her so close only thin cotton separated flesh from flesh. . . .

WHAT ARE *LOVESWEPT* ROMANCES?

They are stories of true romance and touching emotion. We believe those two very important ingredients are constants in our highly sensual and very believable stories in the *LOVESWEPT* line. Our goal is to give you, the reader, stories of consistently high quality that may sometimes make you laugh, sometimes make you cry, but are always fresh and creative and contain many delightful surprises within their pages.

Most romance fans read an enormous number of books. Those they truly love, they keep. Others may be traded with friends and soon forgotten. We hope that each *LOVESWEPT* romance will be a treasure—a "keeper." We will always try to publish

LOVE STORIES YOU'LL NEVER FORGET
BY AUTHORS YOU'LL ALWAYS REMEMBER

The Editors

Linda Cajio
Night Music

BANTAM BOOKS
NEW YORK · TORONTO · LONDON · SYDNEY · AUCKLAND

NIGHT MUSIC

A Bantam Book / November 1991

If you would be interested in receiving protective vinyl
covers for your Loveswept books, please write to this address
for information:

Loveswept
Bantam Books
P.O. Box 985
Hicksville, NY 11802

ISBN 0-553-44196-5

Published simultaneously in the United States and Canada

PRINTED IN THE UNITED STATES OF AMERICA

OPM   0 9 8 7 6 5 4 3 2 1

For Lettice. A writer is blessed when a character like her comes along. I consider myself very blessed. Thanks for the run.

Prologue

It was the family meeting to end all family meetings. Frustrated, annoyed, and generally feeling "we've had enough and we're not taking it anymore," each one of the occupants of the room had come at the first call. Lettice Kitteridge had poked, prodded, and interfered in her grandchildren's lives long enough. They were out for revenge.

"After what she did to Miles and me over my grandfather's will," Catherine Wagner-Kitteridge said, "she has to be taught a lesson about this matchmaking. She went too far this time."

"Absolutely," Ellen Kitteridge-Carlini added. "She threw me at Joe."

"*I* threw me at you," her husband, Joe, said. "Or did you forget the skating rink, El?"

Ellen smiled. "You were in desperate straits."

"And using desperate measures."

"She did a full-blown American invasion on me," Rick Kitteridge said, his English accent noticeably pronounced among his cousins. He and his wife, Jill Daneforth-Kitteridge, had flown over from England especially for this meeting.

"You never would have met me if she hadn't," Jill pointed out. "Think of all the fun we had."

"I could have skipped my brief career as a cat burglar," her husband grumbled.

Jill giggled and whispered something in his ear about nights in white satin.

"She never trusted Remy," Susan Kitteridge-St. Jacques said, interrupting her brother's wife.

"*You* never trusted me, chère," Remy said. "Fortunately it took just one look for me—especially in that bikini you were wearing."

Susan blushed, then chuckled. "Grandmother didn't like that either."

"You all forget that I was subjected to the worst torture of all," Anne Kitteridge-Farraday said. "She moved in with me!"

"Unforgettable," her husband, James, agreed, then added hastily when his wife glared at him, "You, I mean. Not Aunt Lettice."

"Obviously we have all had our share of Lettice's matchmaking attempts," Catherine said, bringing the family conclave back to order. "But the point of this meeting is to stop her before she strikes again."

Devlin Kitteridge studied his sister-in-law as she spoke. Leave it to his brother to marry a beautiful go-getter, he thought. Glancing over at his twin, he had to admit that Miles looked happy enough. But Devlin wasn't there to celebrate the newlyweds' bliss. He was there to get his grandmother off his back. Ever since Miles had married, his grandmother had paraded woman after woman under his nose. She'd even sent them down to his charter-boat business in Wildwood, New Jersey, when he refused to come up to her home in Gladwynne, Pennsylvania. It had reached a point that any time he saw a woman under the age of thirty-five walking on the same side of the street as he, he was certain she'd been sent by Lettice to trap him.

As far as he was concerned, women were only an occasional recreational requirement. Go beyond that and they could break a man. He ought to know. So should his brother. Catherine had jerked Miles's chain countless times, yet the man came back for more. He even called her his earth angel.

Dev grimaced. Obsession could easily turn to tragedy. Quickly, as he had for years, he turned his mind away from that thought and back to the current discussion.

"I have only one question," he said. "*How* are you going to stop her?"

"Worried?" Miles asked, chuckling.

"Annoyed. I'm the only victim left."

"Why don't you find someone for Great-grand-mother?" Anne's son, Philip, asked, having wandered into the room in the middle of the discussion.

In one swift motion all the adults swiveled around to face him.

"I mean . . . she found someone for all of you," he added, looking nervous at the sudden attention. "Maybe if she had someone, she'd be happy and leave everyone alone."

"Out of the mouths of babes," Anne murmured.

"He's a Kitteridge," someone said.

James ruffled his adopted son's hair. "He's a Farraday."

"Any ideas who we could match her up with?" Catherine asked. "All the older gentlemen I know are scared to death of her."

Philip shrugged. So did the rest.

"Wait a minute," James said. "My grandmother told me a long time ago about Aunt Lettice being engaged to someone before she married your grandfather. Something about it being a great tragedy—"

"Call her," Dev snapped impatiently.

James merely looked at him.

"Chill out, big brother," Miles admonished. "Save the orders for your boat."

"You're not her next intended victim," Dev reminded him.

Anne nodded decisively. "Call her," she said to her husband.

"I know, I know," James said. "I got the 'obey' part in my end of the wedding vows." He rose and walked over to the telephone.

He was back a minute later. "Marshall Rayburn."

Joe whistled. "The surgeon? I didn't even know they knew each other."

"Neither did the rest of us." James grinned. "He's a widower."

"Well, well," Miles said.

"There's more." James was laughing now. "He's got a granddaughter, Hilary, who's single. Are you all thinking what I'm thinking?"

Suddenly the very air changed, and Dev, who had been so irritated a moment ago with the slow pace of this meeting, now felt as if his relatives were reading one another's minds at lightning speed.

"It's going to be tricky," Remy said.

"We're going to have to blind-side her," Susan added.

"Is it fair to Dr. Rayburn to saddle him with her?" Rick asked.

"This is no time for a conscience," Jill said. "The

plan's got to be foolproof, because Lettice is no fool."

Ellen laughed. "We're going to sucker-punch her."

Anne joined her. "I love it."

"I think of it more as a merger," Miles said.

"If we play it right, it'll be the coup of the decade," Joe said.

"The century." Catherine rapped on the coffee table. "Then we're all agreed."

"What?" Dev asked. "What the hell are you talking about?"

"You've been away too long," Miles said. "Even Rick, who lives across the ocean, got it. We're going to trick grandmother into being matched with Marshall Rayburn."

"Oh." Dev grinned. "Hell, let's go for it."

"I'm glad you're in agreement. We'll just drop the hint to Grandmother about the granddaughter. You should probably go see Hilary first, to let her know to play along for a dinner or two."

Dev frowned. "What dinner or two?"

They told him. His jaw dropped in astonishment and horror.

"No," he said. "*No! No! No!*"

The family smiled.

One

"Dresden?"

Hilary Rayburn watched Devlin Kitteridge—who looked distinctly out of place in her elegant living room—casually handle her most prized possession, a two-hundred-year-old ceramic shepherdess. "Yes," she replied.

He looked her up and down as if she were a piece of meat in an Armani suit, then set the shepherdess on the glass shelf of the étagère with a clang. "Thought so. They always look as cheap as their knockoffs."

Hilary bit her tongue against a caustic remark. He could be a prospective customer, she told herself, and she couldn't afford to offend any at this point in her business. She tucked her silk scarf higher on her shoulder, then walked over to the étagère and closed and locked the door. Smiling sweetly, she said, "That one survived four border disputes, two revolutions, and two world wars before my grandmother smuggled it out of Hungary. If it looks careworn, it has a right to."

He grinned at her, seeming not at all embarrassed. Hilary knew some members of his family, including his formidable grandmother, but she had only heard about him. And she had heard nothing good. His appearance certainly lived up to his black-sheep reputation. Tall and lean, he was dressed in worn jeans and a maroon polo shirt that had seen better days. His features were all sharp, rugged angles and could have been carved in granite. His skin was darkly tanned, the crow's-feet at his eyes obvious, giving his face an older look. His eyes were a stunning blue-green, the kind of sharp contrasting color that Paul Newman possessed. As those eyes fixed on her, she felt he could easily strip away the social mask she always kept in place, suddenly exposing the real Hilary. She didn't like that notion.

Their gazes still locked, he pushed his hair off his forehead. As she watched his tanned fingers thread through the dark and sun-streaked strands, she wondered if all the air had left the room. She couldn't quite catch her breath. The scent of male and the sea teased her senses, and she felt a primitive awareness course through her bloodstream. At last she realized she was staring at him, and with effort she turned away.

"I'm sorry," she said as she stepped over to a chair and sat down, "but I can only give you about ten minutes, Mr. Kitteridge. I have a dinner engagement."

He frowned. "I didn't drive for two hours just to talk for a few minutes."

"Then you should have called first." She smiled pleasantly, deciding the man was a complete idiot. A good-looking one, though. Her breathing still wasn't back to normal.

"Break the dinner date."

She raised her eyebrows. "I beg your pardon?"

He slouched down on her sofa, his hands in his pockets. "Look, it's important."

"Then I suggest you get started, Mr. Kitteridge."

He gave her a look that could have frozen hell over. She held on to every ounce of her courage against it. She couldn't change her plans, even if she wanted to. And she was damned if she wanted to for an arrogant, egotistical, nasty boy like Devlin Kitteridge. She'd be a fool to agree to work for him. No matter what he paid, it wouldn't be worth it. She opened her mouth to tell him so.

"My grandmother is going to try to match you up with me," he said, then added bluntly, "I want you to go along with it."

Hilary gaped, her mind whirling. "Match us up?"

He made a face. "Yes, like in *Hello, Dolly*. She thinks she's Carol Channing in disguise."

"You . . . and me?" She stared at him, at his disreputable clothes. He must be nuts.

"Yes, you and me. Ludicrous as that sounds."

"This is a joke, right?" she asked.

"I wish." He straightened and rested his forearms on his thighs, his gaze intent on her. "It's simple, really. My grandmother has been making a habit of finding mates for her grandchildren. I'm her last intended victim, and she's driving me crazy with it. My family wants a little revenge by matchmaking her, and I want to be left alone to run my boat charters. My family's discovered your grandfather was once engaged to my grandmother, and they think something could be rekindled. They also think the best way to get the two of them together is through us. I know this sounds like the stupidest thing you've ever heard, because it's the stupidest thing I've ever said."

Hilary sat back in the chair, stunned. Clearly he didn't want a dinner party catered. If she had been asked to guess why the crude, rude Devlin Kitteridge had come to see her, it wouldn't have been this.

A picture of her grandfather came into her mind. He had always been so vital, but ever since her grandmother had died a year ago, he'd changed. He was apathetic now, refusing to go anywhere except to her town house. Instead of gradually coming out of mourning, he was rapidly sinking into real depression. She didn't know how to stop it. But now . . .

She remembered the scrapbook she'd once found in her grandfather's office. It had been filled with clippings of Devlin's grandmother, sixty years' worth. The opportunity was so perfect, she'd be a fool to pass it up. And she'd be a fool to do it too.

Devlin suddenly stood up, waving his hands. "Forget it. This is absurd, and I was absurd to even come here. No way any sane woman would agree—"

"Please. Mr. Kitteridge," she said. "Sit down."

"I'm not a nut," he said, slumping back down on the sofa. "Maybe you know my brother, Miles, and his wife, Catherine? They can vouch for this. But I know it's stupid, so thanks for patiently listening to my family's ravings. . . ."

She knew his brother slightly and knew the two were twins. And, talk about "good twin, bad twin . . ." she thought. Devlin was the exact opposite of Miles, the charming, successful banker.

". . . All we're asking," Devlin was continuing,

"is that you go along with it for a few . . . dates. Just to get the ball rolling."

She tucked the scarf closer around her chest, took a deep breath, looked Mr. Macho-man right in the eye, and said, "All right."

Dev blinked. Of all the answers he'd expected, it wasn't this one.

"You'll do it?" he asked in shock.

She nodded. "Yes."

He couldn't refrain from asking the obvious. "Why?"

"Because I think your family's right about my grandfather and your grandmother. I'm willing to do anything to see him happy."

"Including suffering with me," Dev added, rubbing his unshaven chin. He'd been up since four that morning. Probably he should have shaved before he'd come, but he'd been in a hurry to get the whole business over with.

He glanced at her, irritated by the sleekly tailored suit she was wearing . . . the perfect little scarf tied so perfectly in an intricate knot on her shoulder . . . the shoulder-length hair, whose simple cut probably cost more than his loan payments . . . the flawlessly creamy skin and porcelain features . . . the slender hands with scarlet-tipped nails . . . the full breasts pressing against the suit jacket . . . the thighs enticingly outlined by her slim skirt . . .

He resisted the urge to haul her body against his and find sweet oblivion. He must be nuts to think there'd be any oblivion with Miss Prim. *Ms.* Prim, he corrected himself. She probably took pride in that abbreviation.

She rose to her feet, and he nearly groaned when he saw her skirt was deliciously wrinkled just at the junction of her legs. "If that's all, Mr. Kitteridge, I have to go."

"Yeah, the date." He pushed himself up off the sofa, wondering what jerk she was seeing and whether or not he knew him from the old days. "I expect my grandmother will be calling you soon, once my cousins get it into her head that you and I would be a 'perfect' match."

"Fine," she said, smiling like a robot. "Good-bye, Mr. Kitteridge."

"Dev," he corrected her. "If we're going to be matched, we'll have to act the part."

"Devlin," she conceded.

He looked heavenward. *Perfect opposites,* he thought. Everything about her was everything he'd hated for so long. Too bad it was all attached to a great body.

She led the way to her front door. He followed, loving the way her skirt outlined her hips and thighs. She had one helluva backside. A man would kill to smooth his hands down its soft curve, then slip around to find the lushness beyond. . . .

He nearly bumped into her when she stopped to open the door, and the fantasy burst in a large dose of reality. Still, the scent of her perfume was doing subtle, sensual things to his senses. Okay, so she had great perfume, but that didn't mean he had to be a fool.

He stopped on the threshold. "Look, you don't have to worry that this matchmaking crap will actually work with you and me. I just want my grandmother off my back, and I'm willing to do anything to do it."

"Only a baboon would think we're compatible," she agreed.

She didn't have to put it quite so bluntly, he thought.

"Right," he said, and walked out the door.

It banged shut after him.

As he drove home, two things occurred to him. The first was that she had agreed awfully quickly to the proposition, despite her claim that she wanted to see her grandfather happy. It was enough to make him wary. The second was that he was too damned interested in her date that night. It had been bothering him ever since she'd mentioned it.

A third thought struck him. She had gotten him in and out of the house in eight minutes.

The date must be a hot one.

And he didn't like that at all.

"Hilary Rayburn?" Lettice repeated into the phone, carefully giving her voice the right touch of astonishment. Her granddaughter, Ellen, was completely transparent, she thought. All of her grandchildren were.

"If I were actually looking for someone for Devlin . . . " she continued slowly.

"You are and you know it," Ellen said.

"Maybe. Mmmm. I don't know Hilary very well. But let me think about it."

After she had hung up, Lettice allowed herself to take a deep breath of relief. Sixty years was a long time to love someone. But she had. If only she had been braver. . . .

She hadn't, though, and she could never make up for that. But she could make a new beginning, even as she got the last of her grandchildren settled. Devlin, who clung so tenaciously to his pain, would not be nearly as easy as the others. That was why she'd saved him for last.

Transparent grandchildren. She wondered how far they would go.

She picked up the telephone to find out.

"Dinner at Lettice Kitteridge's?"

Hilary paused in wiping off a counter in her grandfather's kitchen and smiled innocently at him. It had been a week since Devlin Kitteridge's bizarre visit to her home. As he had predicted, his grandmother had called her a few days later to invite her to dinner.

"Nothing formal," Lettice had said, which Hilary knew meant she needn't wear a long gown. "I'm only having a few close friends over. But it will be a wonderful business opportunity for you, Hilary, because I know every one of my friends is desperate to find a new and excellent caterer."

"Sounds like a marvelous idea," Hilary had said. "Thank you for thinking of me, Mrs. Kitteridge."

"'Mrs. Kitteridge'?" Lettice had repeated, sounding amused. "Oh, no, my dear. You must call me Lettice."

And with that she'd said good-bye, and hung up, without once mentioning her grandson.

Now, having idly told her grandfather about her dinner engagement for the following evening, Hilary noted how his fingers tightened around his coffee cup. It was the first sign of emotion she'd seen in months. Certainly it was the first one this night, at one of their regular twice-weekly dinners at his house. Interesting, she thought.

"Yes," she said, "Lettice Kitteridge. How was the orange-poppyseed dressing on the apple salad?"

she added, deliberately changing the subject to see how intrigued he was by her mention of Lettice. "I'm experimenting."

"Almost too sweet. What are you catering for Mrs. Kitteridge?"

Bingo, she thought, smothering a grin. "I'm not catering. She asked me to dinner as a guest."

Her grandfather set his coffee cup down in a too-careful manner. It spoke volumes.

"Moving up in the world, aren't we?"

His tone was nearly as sarcastic as Devlin's, she thought, and that surprised her.

"I thought we were already there," she said.

"Once, maybe. It's amazing to discover what people are really like when you lose all your money."

"That was sixty years ago in the Depression, Grandfather," she reminded him. He was certainly in his cynical mood tonight. "Besides, you made it all back in the pharmaceutical business."

In his first years as a surgeon in the mid-1930s, he had invented a technique using sulfa and antibiotic drugs to make them more effective. He'd sold the technique to the Walters-Stevens Pharmaceutical Company just before World War II began, thereby helping save thousands of lives.

"Yes, I might have made it all back," Marsh said, "but more importantly, I was a better person for it. But now I'm nouveau riche. I get to look at their bladders instead of their Monets."

"That's only because you like their bladders better," she said.

He laughed, and saluted her with his coffee cup.

Her grandfather might still be bitter, Hilary mused as she turned back to her cleaning up, but her mother, if she were there, would be ecstatic about the dinner invitation from Lettice. For as long as Hilary could remember, her parents had moved on the fringes of the old Philadelphia families' intimate social circle, desperately clinging to it, trying to reestablish the Rayburns' position in it, and getting almost nowhere. They tenaciously followed all of the archaic societal rules, even planning vacations around the movements of the best families, rather than their daughter's school schedule. Their annual jaunts to Palm Beach in the winter and Cape Cod in the summer were funded by the generous salary her father received for his mostly figurehead position as a vice president with Walters-Stevens. When Hilary was younger, they had casually left her, their only child, with her paternal grandparents. She'd considered that a much more preferable fate. Life with her parents was rigid with social customs of dos and don'ts, while Marsh and Elise's home was filled with laughter, fun, and love. At least, Hilary thought as she wiped the last counter, she put all the rigmarole—as well as the contacts she made through her parents' avid social climbing—to excellent use with her business.

"This is good coffee," Marsh said, interrupting her musing. "I don't suppose it's out of a jar, like in the commercials."

She raised her eyebrows. "African-grown, and freshly ground right before brewing."

"Don't you ever eat at McDonald's, instead of having this fancy cuisine all the time?"

She laughed. "Once a week, and I've been known to hit a Taco Bell upon occasion. Happy now?"

"Indubitably." He got up, taking his cup with him. "Have fun at the dinner."

Not exactly the response she'd hoped for, Hilary

thought. But there *had* been a definite spark of something.

She still couldn't believe her conversation with Devlin Kitteridge. It felt so unreal. Even more unreal was her willingness to do it. She must be nuts. But her grandfather needed something to snap him out of his fog.

She wondered if she should have told him about Devlin. She had a feeling more than a spark of interest would be the result. It was certainly the result with her. Her reaction to Devlin was dangerous. Maybe she ought to skip the dinner. If she were smart, she would. If she were the perfectly correct daughter her parents had always wanted her to be, she would. But "perfectly correct" had never interested her, and she was intrigued to see just how far Devlin Kitteridge was willing to go to save himself from his grandmother.

After his granddaughter had left, Marshall Rayburn sat down in front of the TV for another mindless round of the boob tube. Lately it appealed to him more than he cared to admit.

He thought of Hilary's surprise announcement that night. He had set Lettice Kitteridge aside decades ago, nurturing his anger and bitterness until Elise had come into his life . . . and until she died. Now that the future was gone, he seemed to prefer being lost in memories of the past. He couldn't stop it. It was the curse of an old man.

Damn that woman, he thought. She was treacherous, fickle. She'd broken their engagement because his family had lost all its money in the 1929 stock market crash. He hadn't forgotten that in sixty years, and he didn't like it at all that Hilary was going to dinner there.

Worse, Hilary had her hopes up. He frowned, wondering why she was so eager. He'd have to keep an eye on her—to keep her from being hurt.

There was no other reason he was interested, Marsh told himself firmly. Absolutely none.

Dev tugged at his tie, silently cursing the restricting noose around his neck. And *noose* was the right word, he thought. He felt hung at this dinner of his grandmother's. Who wouldn't, with eight elderly blue-rinsed ladies sitting around the formally set dining table cackling like scrawny hens in a chicken coop? The food was so rich, it made him ill. The talk was of people he barely remembered and didn't care to know better, and the atmosphere was laden with social-registry etiquette. He hated it. Why the hell had he told his grandmother he'd come to dinner? He should have stayed home on his boat. It was amazing to think that all the shallowness he saw now had once meant everything to him.

And then there was Hilary.

She sat across from him looking poised and serene. Nothing broke through that brittle shell of hers. She could be the all-time queen of the debutantes. She was chatting easily with his grandmother and her friends. In forty years, he guessed, she'd be one of them and just as ludicrous.

Gazing at her, he wondered if the hint of shadow under her pale-yellow silk dress was the aureole of her nipples. He'd been wondering that all evening, ever since she'd walked in the door. Just once he'd like to see her flesh tighten and betray her through the sheer fabric. It would give him satisfaction to know something got through her icy exterior—and he wanted that something to be him. Why? he asked himself. Why her?

He nearly jumped when the lady sitting next to him touched his arm. She was smiling. "I said, I understand from your grandmother that you're a sport fisherman."

"Hell, no, lady," he said, grinning. "I just take those guys out on the *Madeline Jo* and watch 'em puke over the side."

Everyone gasped. He didn't care. This damn dinner was as ridiculous as everything else in the haughty social milieu the Kitteridges were a part of.

"Thank you, Devlin," his grandmother said. "That was most descriptive."

The conversation began again, though he noticed Hilary was gazing at him instead with a faint smile. She was the only one, he realized, who hadn't been shocked by his answer. Finally she lowered her gaze. He watched in fascination as she scooped up some of her parfait dessert. Slowly she licked the creamy froth from the spoon, the action completely unconscious and incredibly sexy. His blood slowed and pounded its way through every inch of his veins. It buzzed loudly in his ears, drowning out the chicken cackle of the older women. Hilary's lips pursed slightly, almost like an invitation, then her tongue touched the corner of her mouth to catch an errant dollop of ice cream. She looked up and caught him staring.

Her eyes widened as she stared back. He couldn't look away. A tenuous thread, invisible but there just the same, seemed to sew itself between them, pulling them together like two pieces of matched fabric.

With a mighty effort he tore his gaze from hers. He was almost panting for breath, and realized his own spoon was poised halfway to his parfait glass. Dammit, he thought, and shoved the spoon into the stiffened cream. He was behaving like a moon-struck ass. No woman should be allowed to exert that much control over a man.

He watched Hilary glance at his spoon, then back to his face. She calmly scooped out another spoonful of her own parfait and ate it. She wasn't even fazed, he realized with growing annoyance.

He caught his grandmother smiling gleefully at him. Obviously she thought things were moving right along at her little matchmaking dinner party. Fury rose up in him at the idea that he was actually responding to this game he and Hilary were playing, and Hilary wasn't.

He decided to teach Ms. Prim Hilary Rayburn a lesson in sexual manners. He smiled charmingly at her and finally took a bite of his dessert. Everything appeared nice and normal.

Under the table was another matter. He slipped off his shoes, then stretched his leg across the space to rub her calf with his foot.

The woman next to Hilary jumped suddenly.

Dev snatched his foot back.

The elderly woman looked at him, then smiled knowingly.

Wonderful, he thought. Now he'd turned on someone old enough to be his grandmother. He kept his head down to hide the heat on his face as he finished his dessert. So much for lessons.

Still, he couldn't resist the temptation. He stretched his leg out again, and this time his aim was true. Hilary's eyes widened the moment his foot slid against her ankle. She glanced up, and he grinned at her.

She never flinched; she just moved her leg away. Other than that one look, she did not reveal any reaction to what he was doing. It made him all the angrier, and he rubbed his foot against her leg again, riding it high on the inside of her calf.

He knew she couldn't move her leg any farther away without everyone discovering what he was doing. It would be interesting to see how she'd handle him this time.

Hilary stared across the table at Devlin Kitteridge, willing herself not to betray the fury inside her. With the dining chairs nearly butted up alongside each other, she had no room to get her legs out of the way, and he knew it. The man was despicable. And if he were a few inches shorter, he'd never be able to do this to her.

His foot slowly caressed her calf, like a leisurely kiss. A sensual heat radiated outward from the source, pulsing along her thighs. She pressed her knees more tightly together to try to rid herself of the unwanted sensation. And to keep him from going any higher.

His foot pushed against her closed knees, attempting to force them open. She kept her gaze straight on his smirking face and let her hand drop below the tabletop. She smiled intimately at him. He smiled back. Then she ever so intimately jabbed him in the foot with her spoon.

Devlin jumped, knocking over his parfait glass. It shattered his empty coffee cup. Too bad, Hilary thought. He needed some cooling off, and scalding-hot coffee would have done the trick.

"Dear, dear," she said.

"Sorry," he apologized, shrugging ungraciously

to his grandmother. He then glared at Hilary. She smiled sweetly.

Lettice reached over and righted his glass. "Dev, why don't you take Hilary out into the garden while I have this cleaned up? Besides, the two of you must be bored to tears with our old-lady conversations."

Her grandson grinned evilly. "Of course."

Hilary repressed a jolt of fear. "It's really cool out tonight, Lettice—"

"Nonsense," Lettice said, waving her hand in dismissal. "It's August."

"Shall we go?" Dev asked with great aplomb as he slipped his shoe back on and stood. Cary Grant couldn't have looked more debonair, he assured himself.

Hilary knew she couldn't make any fuss—not if she wanted any future catering business from these women. And these women could mean *a lot* of business for her. She never should have jabbed Devlin in the first place. It had been too risky. *He* could have made a humiliating fuss, and she could have kissed business good-bye. But she had been too angry with him to do anything but react to him.

She pushed back her chair and stood. "Dinner was lovely, Lettice."

"You probably could have done it better," Lettice said.

Hilary smiled. "Of course."

The other women laughed.

Devlin opened the French doors that led from the dining room to the back terrace. She preceded him out of the room and waited until they were across the terrace and down the steps to the garden before rounding on him.

"Don't ever do that again!"

"But I had to make it look good for my grandmother," he protested innocently, "so she would think I'm interested."

"You paw a woman on her first date?" she asked, astonished.

The moon was full, and it was easy to see his frown. "You've got a lot to learn if you think that was 'pawing,' lady."

"And you've got a lot to learn if you think that wasn't." The man was so crude, it was unbelievable. "Look," she added, "those women in there mean business to me—"

"No kidding. But if you think they'll let a social climber like you into the inner circle—"

"Social climber!" she exclaimed. She nearly added that he had her confused with her parents, but bit back the retort. She refused to give him any more ammunition. "I mean the catering business, you dolt!" She spun on her heel and strode away from him, furious at his accusation.

He caught up with her. "Catering? What the hell are you talking about?"

"I have a catering business," she said. "I do dinner parties, private luncheons. That kind of thing."

"A froufrou," he said.

She stopped. "What?"

"You've got a froufrou business. Something to keep you busy so you don't live off Daddy's money."

Hilary refrained from punching him. It wasn't polite to punch your hostess's grandson. All the etiquette books said so. "You are a crude, egotistical, Neanderthal snob."

"And you are a prissy, cold, social-climbing clinging vine," he retorted.

She smiled grimly. "Now that we've cleared the

air. . . . If you pull another stunt like that again, I will quit this whole ridiculous scheme."

"Not if you want your grandfather happy, you won't."

She paused, then came back with her own ammunition. "And do you want your grandmother off your back?"

It was his turn to pause. "Yes."

"Then you will play by the rules. Are we understood?"

He grinned. "Perfectly."

Hilary relaxed slightly. "Good. Now, let's just go back inside and get the rest of the evening over with. Okay?"

"Okay."

They walked back to the house in silence. Hilary forced away the anger that had arisen in her from his comments. She shouldn't care what Devlin Kitteridge thought of her. He was a reverse snob, the worst kind.

They reached the French doors. Through the sheer curtain, she could see the women still at the table, talking. She groaned silently. They had already talked so much, her head ached from listening. But that was part of her business unfortunately. If she didn't project the social graces all the time, no one would trust her to put together a proper social occasion. Ergo, no business. She was beginning to wonder if she'd lost track of the real Hilary behind the socially polite and correct facade.

"Still yakking," Dev said.

She nodded.

"Well, we'd better get going on scene two," he added—and pulled her into his arms.

Two

Dev swiftly lowered his head and captured her lips. They were softer than he'd expected, more full and more sweet. She grabbed his arms and tried to push him away, but he kept her tight against him.

The resistance she was putting up couldn't mask the unique feel of her. Her breasts and thighs branded his body, giving him a breathtaking taste of what she could do to a man if she weren't so damn prissy.

She twisted her head away, breaking the kiss. Her body wiggled against his as she struggled, wreaking havoc with his equilibrium. He gritted his teeth against the sensual onslaught heating his blood.

"What the hell do you think you're doing?" she demanded.

He tightened his hold on her, stopping her arousing wriggling. "Playing for the camera. There are eight pairs of eyes watching us. Don't you want to look like we're getting along?"

"No. Let me go!"

"Hilary, you've got to do better than this if you want my grandmother to get together with your grandfather."

"I'll lock them in a closet," she snapped. "Damn you, you promised you'd be a gentleman."

He chuckled. Her nails were digging into his skin, despite the protection of his jacket and shirt sleeves. They felt almost good. And he couldn't blame her for being angry with him—again. He was acting like an obnoxious oaf, but he wanted to break through that social mask of hers. "My hands are on your back," he said, "not where they'd really like to be. This is as gentlemanly as I get. We've got to do a little playacting for our audience, to show my grandmother her matchmaking is working."

Abruptly Hilary stopped struggling.

If her body squirming against his drove him to the brink, what it did relaxing against his was unprintable. This matchmaking could be more fun that he'd thought, Dev mused. "Anybody ever tell you you've got a body that won't quit?"

"Billy Idol. You've proven your point to the 'audience.' Now, let me go."

She was quick. He liked that. And she had jabbed him with her spoon, revealing an unexpected side to her that he'd like to explore further.

"In a minute," he said.

He continued to hold her close as he gazed down at her, hoping to make her blink first. She stared right back, waiting for him to let her go. He felt something within him responding to her, dragging him forward. The control he'd felt throughout their kiss dissipated. He felt . . . ashamed that he'd kissed her the way he had . . . ashamed that he hadn't cared about her feelings. The notion was disturbing, and he released her abruptly, all but pushing her away in an effort to shake the sensation of vulnerability running through him.

She stumbled backward, and he grabbed her arm. She steadied herself, then stared pointedly at his hand. He let her go. With one hand she smoothed her hair back into place.

"Don't worry," he muttered. "I didn't muss it. No one would know you were kissed. Believe me."

She looked at him strangely, and he wondered why his actions and emotions were so inconsistent. He didn't like her. She represented everything he hated. And she made it obvious the feeling was mutual.

"Shall we go in?" she asked.

"Yeah. What the hell." He opened the door for her, and she slipped inside gracefully. He strolled in after her, hands in his pockets.

"Back already?" Lettice asked, smiling smugly. The rest of her cronies were beaming like neon lights. They hadn't missed the performance. "Didn't you show her the garden, Devlin? It's my pride and joy."

He shrugged. "We saw it."

"It was lovely," Hilary added.

Dev snorted, amused by the contrast between her polite compliment and the way she looked. In the light it was easy to see the soft swelling of her mouth. Makeup was not responsible for either the redness of her lips or the flush on her cheeks. They were only the outward signs, though, he reminded himself. Inside, the freeze was still on. He bet she wasn't capable of thawing.

A restlessness he didn't understand welled up inside him, and he couldn't stand all this nonsense any longer. "Thanks for dinner, Grandmother."

He turned on his heel and strode out the French doors, slamming them shut behind him. The glass panes rattled ominously.

The long ride home to Wildwood didn't rid him of his strange anxiety, and he headed straight to the docks on the bay. The *Madeline Jo* was berthed in the last slip, forty feet of gleaming white and brass. In the darkness he climbed aboard and slipped the ropes off the pilings, then pushed the boat away from the dock.

Once above in the pilot's cabin, he turned the key in the ignition. The engines rumbled to life, and the *Madeline Jo* floated like a ghost across the water. It was insane to take a boat out in the dead of night, but he didn't care. It didn't matter, either, that he had a fishing charter at six the next morning.

He had to work off Hilary Rayburn before she got any farther under his skin.

Out on the water, though, painful memories came back. Memories he hadn't allowed in years and yet lived with every day. Memories of the spring his senior year in college. He'd thought he was invincible then. He'd thought he could do anything. He'd had money, power, a family name that all the right people recognized instantly. And he'd been obsessed with his best friend's fiancée.

He'd wanted Madeline Joanne Belford from the first moment he'd seen her. She was beautiful, and she knew it. And she was Christopher's. That she didn't pay quite as much attention to. Dev had tried to deny himself, tried to stay away, but she had been just as irresistibly attracted to him. Whenever they'd stolen a moment alone together, they'd been all over each other. He'd begged her to break it off with Chris, but she'd delayed, not wanting to hurt him. Dev hadn't wanted to hurt Chris, either, so he'd remained silent, waiting for the "right" moment. His guilt over betraying his friend had been tremendous, and so had the jealousy whenever he'd had to watch Madeline with Chris. She'd seemed to thrive on having the two of them in the same room with her, one touching, caressing, and the other looking on silently.

That should have been his clue, Dev thought. Instead he'd come to hate his best friend. He'd constantly wished Chris out of the picture, so that his way would be clear to Madeline. He got his wish one night in a car. The three of them, Madeline between them as always, teasing Chris and infuriating Dev as he drove.

Dev took a deep, shuddering breath and swiped at the wetness on his face. He could never be sure whether he'd missed seeing the Stop sign . . . or if he had run it deliberately in a moment of unconscious evil. He did know he never saw the truck that broadsided them. He'd suffered multiple bruises and cuts; Madeline had broken a leg and an arm . . . and Chris had been killed.

That one moment changed Dev forever. Madeline got over Chris's death quickly and seemed to want Dev to take his place. But Dev was consumed by guilt. It took him a long time to realize how Madeline had played him off Chris to feed her own ego. He had been too young and too inexperienced to recognize what she was doing. The guilt opened his eyes to his own lifestyle, too, allowing him to see how shallow his life was. So he chucked it all, avoiding his family because he believed they were all shallow as well, traveling around and drifting from job to job, until he settled in Wildwood and bought the *Madeline Jo*. He'd named the boat such to remind him of his foolishness and folly, especially with women. His life had been peaceful ever since. At least he could nearly live with himself most days.

Somehow Hilary Rayburn now threatened his banal existence. He couldn't put his finger on it, but something about her bothered him more than he cared to admit.

Dolphins broke the water several hundred yards out from the boat. Like dark arrows, they leaped and plunged into the black waves. Dev watched them for a moment, then realized the sky was lighter. The fishing charter would be on the dock already, five guys waiting impatiently to catch blues and tunas and maybe a shark.

With a sigh he turned the boat around and headed in.

"So, how was the great dinner the other night?" Marsh asked as soon as he walked in the door of Hilary's town house.

"Fine," Hilary lied, smiling brightly at her grandfather. She fluffed up the bouquet of roses in a vase on the hallway table. Her grandfather didn't even glance at them as he set his driving cap on her hat rack. She'd actually gotten him to her house for lunch, and the flowers were part of her scheme. She primped the pink buds yet again. "Her grandson was there."

Instantly Dev's image—which she had managed to hold at bay the past few days—flashed into her mind. She still couldn't believe the absurd things she'd done at the dinner. First she'd stabbed him with her spoon, then, like an outraged virgin, she'd screeched at him, "Let me go, you brute!" or words to that effect. She'd never been so foolish or so angry . . . and she'd never been kissed like that before. His mouth had been like fire, all sudden heat. She could still feel the hard muscles of his arms under her hands. Every inch of him had been tight against her, fitting perfectly. . . .

She had never been so humiliated, either, at the way he'd abruptly left the dinner, leaving her to face those old biddies alone. But at the end of the evening she had sensed a loneliness in Lettice, and she was determined to salvage something out of the disaster for her grandfather's sake.

"Her grandson?" Marsh asked. "The banker?"

Hilary grinned. "No, the black sheep. Devlin. He lives down by the shore, I believe."

Marsh snorted. "Ran away years ago, after that accident. The only smart one, I'd say."

Her grandfather was nearly as snobbish as Devlin was in his way, Hilary thought, but one thing he'd said certainly perked her interest. "What accident?"

"A car accident when he was in college. He was joyriding or drag-racing, and a boy was killed." Marsh shrugged. "I don't remember the details."

Hilary stared at her grandfather, her mind whirling at this sudden news. "Oh. Well. He sent me these flowers. Aren't they—"

"*He what?*" Marsh roared in a voice that should have shaken the rafters.

Hilary swallowed. This was quite a change from his usual lethargy. "The roses—"

"Don't you go getting involved with those Kitteridges!" her grandfather snapped. "And you stay the hell away from the black sheep! The Kitteridges are treacherous and untrustworthy snobs who consider only themselves—"

"Grandfather," she interrupted. "Lettice was extremely kind to me, and Devlin was a . . . gentleman. You make it sound like we're back in the Middle Ages or something. I'm twenty-eight, with my own business—"

"Then act as smart as you ought to be!"

She blinked. She hadn't seen her grandfather this angry about anything in her entire life. Or this alive. "I am smart, Grand—"

"Not at this!" He glared at her, his jaw working. "I forbid you to see this grandson."

Her jaw dropped at the ultimatum, then she snorted in amusement. "Get real, Grandfather. We are not the House of Capulet."

The doorbell rang, and she spun around to answer it. Saved, she thought as she opened the door.

Devlin stood on her threshold.

Doomed, she thought. She was about to be caught in her little white lie, which had been designed only to tease her grandfather's interest. With him now spouting off, she didn't want to know what Devlin would think.

"Hello," he said.

Her face heated as his deep voice instantly recalled for her the feel of his mouth on hers. She forced away the thought of how she had made a fool of herself with him, and how he had left her hanging. "Hello," she managed to say politely.

"Who is it?" her grandfather asked, coming up behind her.

Devlin smiled and thrust out his hand. "Hello, sir. I'm Devlin Kitteridge. You must be—"

"That's it!" Marsh shouted, and shoved past Devlin right out the door.

". . . Hilary's grandfather," Devlin finished.

Hilary watched her grandfather get into his car, slam the door shut, and zoom out of the parking space. She closed her eyes and groaned. He probably thought she'd arranged the lunch so that he could meet Devlin. What a mess.

"He's nearly as polite as I am," Dev commented.

"What do you want?" she asked in a tired voice, opening her eyes.

"Did you forget to take a 'politeness' pill too?" He eyed her for a moment. "Or did I interrupt something?"

"Just the modern version of *Romeo and Juliet*," she replied. "What do you want?"

He grinned. "I take it I'm Romeo?"

"That's a hoot," she snapped, angry at her own analogy. She should have said *Fatal Attraction*. Devlin Kitteridge was turning out to be the kiss of death for her. "Are you going to tell me what you want, or are you going to play twenty questions?"

"The latter's more fun." He shrugged, shifting his weight onto one leg at the same time. The simple gestures did things to his body, things she didn't want to see. But how could she miss them, when his dark T-shirt clung so to his broad shoulders and chest, and his faded jeans faithfully outlined the shape of his hips and thighs? "I came here," he went on, "to see if you were still going to go on with the plan. I . . . ah, I wasn't fair with you that night at my grandmother's."

It was the best concession she would get from him that he had acted wrongly, Hilary realized. Her grandfather's words about a car accident came back to her. That explained a little about the rude, cynical man before her. But it didn't excuse him. "Okay," she said.

He raised his eyebrows. "That's it? Just okay?"

"What would you like me to say?" she asked, suddenly annoyed with him. "That I'm so thrilled to forgive you for making me look like a fool? You've apologized about as well as you're ever going to, so okay."

He scowled. "I just wanted to make it clear that I kissed you for my grandmother's sake."

An odd pain knifed through her. "I understand. Believe me, I understand."

"The old ladies . . . my grandmother's friends . . . they ticked me off." He shrugged again. "I couldn't stand the cackling any longer, and I had an early charter in the morning. That's why I left the way I did."

He'd driven eighty miles to make it clear his abrupt leaving had had nothing to do with her or with the kiss, Hilary thought. He didn't have to bludgeon her with it, though. "I see. Thank you for telling me."

"So, will you still go along with the game?"

She was silent. Every nerve ending in her body seemed to scream out for him to touch her again, kiss her again as only he could. Common sense instantly countered that, telling her to stay away from him, as far away as possible. But her grandfather's reaction was all too clear. "I've been forbidden to see you."

"You've been—" Devlin frowned, then turned to look at the parking space her grandfather had vacated. When he turned back, he was grinning. "Where there's anger, there's passion."

Hilary couldn't help smiling too. "That's what I was thinking."

"So, we continue the play."

She nodded. "We continue."

His grin turned lethal as he leaned casually against the doorjamb. "How about if I come in and we discuss this further?"

It took her three slow, pounding heartbeats to find her breath. "The game is only in play when we are in front of the grandparents. You get your grandmother to arrange something, then call me."

She had the great satisfaction of closing the door on his dumbfounded expression. One up, she thought, and went into the kitchen for her yellow-fin-tuna-and-wilted-lettuce salad.

No sense letting a good meal go to waste.

Marsh sped along the circular drive toward the fieldstone house he'd never wanted to see. But he'd be damned if this family would swallow Hilary alive and spit her out again half-dead, as it had done to him.

He slammed on the brakes and got out of the car. Jamming his cap down over his eyes, he strode toward the front door.

"Did you want something, Marsh?"

He spun around. Lettice stood on the other side of the drive, a basket filled with fresh-cut flowers on one arm. All the anger swept out of him, and all the memories swept in. He had first seen her at the 1929 Assembly Ball. Small and trim she had been, all of nineteen with dark, dark hair, delicate features, a peaches-and-cream complexion, a stubborn set to her jaw, and the most provocative blue-green eyes. He'd gone dizzy in the head the instant he'd seen her.

Her hair was silver now, but she was still the

same after sixty-one years. And she still made him dizzy in the head.

Marsh forced away the grayness. She looked as unsettled as a stone lion. Clearly his presence didn't affect her the way hers did him. He walked over to her, towering above her as he always had. "You leave my granddaughter alone."

Lettice raised her eyebrows. "I've done nothing with her."

"Your grandson!" Marsh snapped, trying to dispel the sudden notion that he was being a fool. "He'll not do to Hilary what you did to me."

Lettice looked away, then back at him. "That was a long time ago."

"Sixty years," he reminded her. "You weren't there when I needed you the most."

She adjusted the flowers in her basket. "I was young and too scared to go against my parents."

"You didn't love me enough to be poor and unaccepted." He smiled grimly. "I found someone who did."

She lifted her head to meet his gaze. "I was sorry to hear of her passing."

She sounded sincere. He gritted his teeth and nodded.

"What my grandson does," she went on, "and what your granddaughter does is not my business. I don't interfere. Neither should you."

"I won't, as long as you keep him away from her. Or I'll come after you with everything I've got."

"In a pig's eye!" she snapped. "You leave those two alone, Marshall Rayburn."

"I will if they'll leave each other alone. You understand me, Lettice?"

He turned and stalked back to his car, not

waiting for an answer. The tires spun rubber, mirroring his fury as he drove away.

He was still tall and thin, Lettice thought as his car disappeared around the curve in the drive. Almost too thin, she decided. It had been a shock to see him get out of the car. Thank goodness she'd had a moment to compose herself before speaking.

He hated her.

She drew in a deep breath against the pain in her chest. A heart attack would be preferable to the ache she was suffering now. She should have learned to live with it. Usually she did. She had loved Marshall Rayburn as she had loved no other, and she'd told him the truth. She had been too afraid to go against her parents and her upbringing when his family lost everything in the Crash. Life had been full of rules and values and expectations then, to which one was supposed to adhere. Rebellion was not fashionable. If she had been older. . . . She often wondered about that.

No sooner did Marsh's car disappear in one direction than another car came roaring up the drive. Devlin braked his Corvette to a screeching halt. The car door whipped open, and he got out. His expression was thunderous.

"Surprise, surprise," Lettice said, smiling at her usually very absent grandson. "Did the sea finally spit you back out?"

"I want lunch, and then I'm going the hell home," he said in a tone that brooked no argument. "And I don't want a lot of grief while I'm here."

She raised her brows. "Then I suggest you go find the nearest Burger King."

She walked across the driveway and around the

rear of his car, as far away from her glaring grandson as she could get. She wasn't a fool.

"She shut the damn door right in my face," he said suddenly.

Lettice turned around. "I see. You'd better come in for some lunch, then."

"Thanks." He strode past her and on into the house. The fury in him was so obvious, she wouldn't be surprised if he started breathing fire.

Two angry men, she thought.

Her plans were moving along nicely.

Dev knocked on the door at the elegant Radnor town house. He almost couldn't believe he was back here again. He had meant to go straight home after lunch with his grandmother. But stopping to leave a message was cheaper than calling, he told himself.

The door opened, and Hilary stood before him again. The severe white dress she was wearing made her look as polished as an objet d'art—and about as warm. Yet at second glance he realized the dress, as simple as it was, left no doubt that she possessed a body with curves to delight a man. Her stunned expression pleased him too. He needed a little control with her.

"My grandmother will be at some benefit for your grandfather's hospital on Sunday," he said, giving her no chance to recover her icy reserve. "An afternoon tea or something. Will he be there?"

She frowned. "I don't know. He used to go, but lately—"

"Well, get him there," Dev ordered.

Her lips thinned. "I don't *get* anyone anywhere."

"You'd better." He grinned. "If the two of them

don't get together, you and I are stuck playing Romeo and Juliet."

"Heaven forbid," she replied.

Irritation rose up in him at her ready agreement. He forced it back down beneath the surface. What the hell should he care, anyway? They had about as much in common as a pig and a snail.

"Maybe we'd better get some kind of plan together," he began, stepping forward. "So that we know what we're doing."

She put her hand out, stopping him. "I can't right now. I have an engagement shortly."

He scowled. "Break it."

"No!" she snapped, her eyes blazing and her cheeks darkening. "Get a life, Devlin."

"Listen," he said, glaring back at her, "I don't have time to screw around over this, let alone waste time because *you're* some social flitting butterfly. I have a charter to run."

She waved her hand toward his car. "Then go run it! Nobody's stopping you."

She shut the door so fast, he had to jump out of the way or lose several toes. The solid-steel barrier was in his face. Again.

His blood boiled hot and the anger spilled over. He cursed fervently, spinning toward his car.

That was it. Ms. Prim was about to get a lesson she'd never forget.

And she'd never shut him out again either.

Three _____

"I don't see why I have to go to to this."

Hilary glanced over at her grandfather, noting his set jaw and crossed arms. She was a little surprised she'd actually gotten him this far. It had taken three days of continual arguing, pleading, and begging—on both sides. She pulled onto the grassy meadow at the Greenways Country Club, which had been set aside for parking, and said one last time, "It's your hospital. I would think you'd want to support it."

"I'll send them a check," he said, as she'd known he would.

"It's for a good cause, the new pediatric surgery wing," she replied automatically. "Which you *fought* for, before Grandmother died and you took to hiding from the world with this self-indulgent, maudlin garbage. She wouldn't like it, you know."

He frowned at her. "You're becoming a guilt-riding hag, you know that?"

"Thank you. I love you too." Hilary sighed to herself. Getting him there was about all she'd gotten. On the other hand, she thought, brightening, that was the only thing required. "If it will make you any happier, just think of it as a prime opportunity for me to drum up business. There are a hundred clients here who are just waiting for me to walk in and save their dinner parties."

Marsh grinned. "I wondered why you were so insistent on coming."

"And now you know."

He straightened his tie. "Then shall we indulge ourselves at this afternoon tea in the park?"

She grabbed her white gauze picture hat from the backseat and set it carefully on her head. "It's showtime."

Her grandfather chuckled. "Nobody would ever guess what the real Hilary beneath that facade is like."

Hilary wondered, as she often had in the past few months, if the "real Hilary" was still there. She seemed to get lost a little too often in the course of business. Then she thought of how Devlin Kitteridge, seemingly without effort, got right past her well-constructed facade. With effort, she forced his image away and reminded herself of one advantage to this day. Devlin Kitteridge wouldn't be there.

She and her grandfather got out of her car and strolled toward the large tent that dominated the back lawn of the country club.

"This reminds me of times long past," Marsh said, squinting against the bright August sunlight. "The women in filmy tea gowns and the men in white flannels. At least the day is breezy, not that humid muck we usually get in August."

"See? It's not so bad." She tucked her hand

around her grandfather's elbow, smiling to herself as she did. He was in for a big surprise.

"Hello, darling. You look beautiful." The unexpected words were followed by Devlin ducking his head beneath the brim of her hat and kissing her on the cheek.

Hilary gaped at him as he straightened. Beelzebub couldn't have appeared this fast. He looked impeccable in a blue blazer and white flannels. "What are you doing here?" she asked ungraciously when she finally found her voice.

He raised his eyebrows. "Don't tell me you forgot I was coming." He turned to her grandfather and held out his hand, flawlessly covering the older man's temper tantrum of the other day. "I believe we missed being introduced last time. I'm Devlin Kitteridge."

Hilary gaped again. This was the same Devlin of "watch 'em puke" fame?

Marsh's lips had tightened to a thin line. Grudgingly he took Devlin's hand and shook it. "I know who you are. You look like your . . . grandfather."

Devlin nodded. "Others have said that."

"I see some people I should talk with," Marsh said to Hilary. "Will you excuse me?"

Hilary racked her brain for a protest. The last thing she wanted was to be left alone with this changeling. Maybe this was really Miles filling in for his brother. That would explain a lot.

"Of course," Devlin said. To her, he added, "Would you like some champagne, darling?"

Her grandfather stomped away at the endearment. Off to a great start, Hilary thought worriedly. Remembering their "business opportunity" conversation in the car, she figured her grandfather thought she was a liar of the first water.

"Get with the program, woman," Devlin muttered to her as he pulled her in the opposite direction. His hand was like an iron band around her upper arm. "If we're to be believable, you've got to act the part."

"What are you talking about?" she demanded, pulling up short. At least, she thought ruefully, she now knew she was with the "real Devlin." "What program? What *are* you doing here?"

He made a face. "Playing this stupid matchmaking business to the hilt. What did you think?"

"That you weren't coming." She glanced around at the crowd. Devlin had hauled her to the outer edges of it. "Where's your grandmother? If I got him out for nothing—"

"She's here, don't worry." He looked around. "Somewhere. Of course I was coming. I even wanted to talk to you about it when I stopped by your house the other day."

She frowned, remembering that conversation clearly. She ought to; she'd actually managed to get away with her control intact. "You said if I got him here, we wouldn't have to act . . . interested in each other anymore."

"Eventually. Obviously your grandfather doesn't like us together, so obviously he'll come out to try to stop us. Just as obviously my grandmother wants us together. And just as obviously she'll come out to see that we are. Don't you have a brain?"

She smiled sweetly. "Yes, and it's well used too."

"Could have fooled me." He grimaced. "Let's leave the barb trading to a minimum, okay? If we don't act interested in each other, we'll never convince my grandmother or your grandfather that something's going on."

She gazed at his handsome, rugged face with its cynical expression. His expensive clothes accentuated the lines of his lean body almost as well as his faded jeans did. Thinking of his body made her all too aware of the few inches separating them. His cologne mingled with his natural, musky scent, enticing her senses. He was extremely attractive . . . and extremely dangerous.

"I suppose I could force myself to fake it," she said, her squeaking voice betraying her agitation.

He took her hand and pulled her against him so abruptly, she couldn't even gasp for breath. Every inch of him was pressed intimately to every inch of her. Her body heated instantly, and so did her face at the thought of people seeing them like this.

"By the time I get through, Hilary Rayburn, you won't even know what *force* means."

"Get real, Devlin," she said, trying to ignore the quick pounding of her heart. "Your track record so far consists only of Neanderthal tactics. You can't even do it now without a little macho indulgence. Will you let me go?"

He stared at her, then smiled a slow, leisurely smile. The air seemed to whoosh out of her already-constricted lungs. But he let her go.

"You could use a little macho indulgence," he said, courteously holding out his arm to her.

She tucked her hand around his elbow, then leaned close to him. "What I could use," she murmured, "you don't have."

The fingers of his other hand wrapped warmly around hers as they began to stroll together. She felt the touch shudder through her.

"If you think that," he replied, tilting his head down to hers, "then you're about to be surprised . . . darling."

She eased away from him as much as she could. "Don't flatter yourself. And call me darling or anything resembling that word again and you'll be looking at your back teeth. Understand?"

He chuckled. "I think I'm beginning to like you, Hilary."

She smiled, feeling strangely exhilarated. "Heaven forbid."

He patted her hand. "Come on. Let's go steal some champagne."

Marsh watched his granddaughter lean forward and whisper something intimate to Devlin Kitteridge. He hadn't missed their short embrace a moment earlier either. They were oblivious to everything around them. The attraction between the young couple was so tangible, he could almost reach out and touch it.

He remembered all too well when he and Lettice had acted similarly. The thought left him feeling ill.

"They make a handsome couple, don't you think?"

Lettice's voice plunged through him like a shock of cold water. He hadn't heard her come up. Maybe it was time for a hearing aid.

Somehow, though, a part of him wasn't surprised by her presence. A vague expectation was now satisfied.

"No," he said, looking straight at her.

"Liar," she replied softly.

Not much ever fooled her, he thought. She looked very beautiful in a lavender lace coat with a matching dress underneath. Silver hair peeked out from beneath her picture hat. The color was still a shock for him.

"You must be proud of the turnout today," she added, when he didn't respond to her barb. "After all, this is your wing."

"The hospital's wing, not mine."

"You started it, I understand."

He shrugged. "I'm surprised you don't have all the dirt. You used to."

"I still hear a thing or two. You look well after all these years," she said. "I didn't get a chance to tell you that the other day. You were too busy being the outraged grandfather."

"I still am," he told her. "But I know when I've been outmaneuvered, and I'm just not going to kick up a fuss in front of others."

"You can't stop them or what they feel, Marsh."

"*You* stopped fast enough," he snapped. "You turned it off the moment I lost everything . . . and then turned it right back on with Kitteridge."

She stared at him for one long, endless moment, then walked away.

"I didn't think you really meant it," Hilary said.

Dev grinned as he poured champagne into two plastic glasses. He'd casually filched the bottle out of the ice tub when the bartender had been busy. He didn't bother to tell Hilary he'd left more than enough money in its place. "How else did you think we were going to get a whole bottle of the stuff?"

"Ask?"

He chuckled. "That's no fun."

She leaned back against the trunk of the huge oak tree they were sitting under. The small, crowded-together wrought-iron tables hadn't appealed to them, so they'd strolled farther out into the meadow.

To Dev's own surprise, he'd been a gentleman and spread his coat out for her to sit on. Lucky coat, he thought, eyeing the way her slim thighs melded into the material. Her dress was a soft and filmy cotton that clung in all the right places, with a low-cut scoop neckline and a white collar. She looked like a modern Gibson Girl.

She held her stemmed glass up and eyed it. "It's a sacrilege to put champagne in plastic."

He held up the bottle. "It's cheap champagne."

"Oh. Well, that's okay, then." She swallowed it down in one gulp, then shivered. "Lord. It's like drinking vinegar and bad tonic water."

He raised his eyebrows. "Do you always drink champagne like that?"

"Only the cheap stuff."

"I see." He poured her another glass. It would be interesting to see Ms. Prim a little tipsy, he thought as he took a careful sip of his own. She was right on the money about the taste.

"I'm surprised you're not on your boat today," she said. "What happened? No charter?"

"There's always a charter." He rested his arms on his bent knees, his glass dangling precariously in his hands. "Billy took the *Madeline Jo* today." He frowned darkly. "And he damn well better bring her in without a scratch."

"I take it Billy is your first mate?"

"And general swabbie." Dev shrugged off the worry. There was no sense to it while he was stuck here. Unfortunately sitting there with Hilary didn't feel like "stuck."

"Billy sounds young," she said.

Dev chuckled. "Billy's a retired accountant. This

fills the days, I guess. I'm grateful for him, but I wish he was more forceful at times."

"What do you mean?"

"I have one rule for my charters. No booze, no drugs, and no women unless they're wives. All three are trouble I don't need. Billy hates to be the bad guy by telling them no."

She raised her eyebrows. "Why make an exception for wives? I would think a machismo captain like you wouldn't want *any* women on board."

"Wives, dear lady, are the only women who are serious about the fishing when they're with the men, so I allow them. Other women are too busy turning on the sex appeal in front of the men, and the men are too busy paying attention to them instead of the fish. They can do the same thing in the lobby of the Taj Mahal. I'm not a floating hotel."

She grinned. "But you are a male chauvinist."

"Thank you."

"You sound like you love your boat very much."

He smiled. "She's the best thing that ever happened to me."

"Ahh, I see." She nodded knowingly. "Far more than a boat, slightly less than a mistress."

He laughed at her description. "Close. I also have a silent partnership in a cruise ferry for gamblers between Wildwood and Atlantic City. That one I leave to my partner. But I love being on the water. You never know what will pop up—"

"Such as Jaws," she broke in.

"Or a pod of whales or a school of dolphins or a sudden squall." He gazed at her. "Anything can be out there, and you're in something that's about the size of a peanut, challenging it."

She glanced down at her glass. "Your boat has a pretty name."

He looked away. "Yes."

She said nothing more, and he wondered if she knew about the accident. He couldn't imagine that she didn't. Nobody let a scandal lie sleeping as it should, but he was grateful she hadn't mentioned it or asked about it. Hilary Rayburn went up a few points in his estimation. He glanced at her glass. It was still full. "Aren't you drinking?"

She grinned at him. "Not if I can help it."

"I could try to steal a better brand this time."

"Maybe later."

He swallowed the last of his champagne and poured himself some more. "So, why aren't you attached to anyone?"

"I've got you," she reminded him.

"Thrill of thrills, I'm sure. I meant a real man."

She smothered a laugh. "Makes me wonder what you are, then." Before he could respond, she shrugged and said, "I lived with a man for a while."

It was his turn to raise his eyebrows. Prim and proper Hilary Rayburn had lived in sin? "What happened to him? Did he 'do you wrong'?"

"No. I done him wrong." She looked away.

Dev gaped. "You cheated on him?"

She turned back. "Of course not! Whatever gave you that ridiculous idea?"

One look at her honey-brown hair and the lush curves that made a man ache to touch her and Dev knew it wasn't a ridiculous idea at all. "You said you done him wrong. Don't you ever listen to Billie Holiday or Bessie Smith?"

"I'm more Harry Connick, Jr., and The Moody Blues."

"Harry's got potential, but The Moody Blues are the wrong kind. I'll lend you some of my *real* blues albums. So, what did you do?"

"I . . ." She took a deep breath, and he nearly choked at the way her breasts pressed against the sheer fabric of her bodice. "I didn't love him."

Her words confirmed his first impressions of her: cold as ice and about as emotional as a robot. Somehow it pained him to realize it was true. At least she knew it about herself, he admitted.

"I was too young, really," she went on, twirling the stem of her glass. "Sometimes we do things when we're young on an impulse or because we think it's a good idea, and then we realize afterward it's not."

Dev looked out over the green grass. "I know."

"He deserved someone who did love him, wonderfully and with her whole heart. I wasn't that person, so I told him he should go find her. It seemed only right." A ripple chased down her body, as if she were shaking cobwebs out of an old blanket. Then she smiled. "Well, anyway, I still have you. Thrill of thrills."

He grinned as she tossed his own words back at him. This day had started out as a torture, until this enlightening conversation. Just when he thought there were no surprises left, she surprised him. There was a lot of Hilary under the social mask she always had on. How could she be this warm and teasing and yet be so cold inside? Or was she?

An urge rose up in him, gentle but overwhelming. He leaned toward her, his gaze never wavering. Neither did hers. Their lips met. The kiss was sweet and tender, their mouths caressing each other's. Everything inside him went gray, a soft kaleidoscope of gray. He pressed slightly, and her lips parted under his touch. Their tongues swirled leisurely together. He was afraid to touch her anywhere else, afraid of what he would find. Her mouth tasted of the finest champagne, yet more heady and more sensual. His body had no air, nothing to breathe but her. He felt as if he were falling into a warm abyss, from which he never wanted to emerge.

They pulled away at the same time, as if she felt that final plunge into the nothingness exactly when he did. He stared at her in shock. She stared back, her eyes wide. He wanted to deny the tender, alien sensations running through him. He didn't want soft, or sweet, or intimate from her.

He turned and again looked out over the meadow, trying to regain his equilibrium. He was conscious that she did the same. He wanted to say something cynical or witty or even obnoxious, but he couldn't find words. His mind was too filled with only one thought.

If Hilary Rayburn was a cold woman, where had that kiss come from?

Seated at one of the tables, Lettice watched her grandson kiss Hilary. Clearly things were going on that Devlin hadn't planned. She smiled to herself. It served her grandson right.

Out of the corner of her eye she saw Marsh striding toward the younger couple. She immediately rose from her chair and started on a collision course toward him. Things might not be going quite so well with him, but she wasn't about to allow him to ruin Devlin and Hilary.

She cut him off before he reached the couple and planted herself directly in his path. "Some of the hospital people are looking for you, Marsh."

He pulled up short and blinked. She took him by

the elbow, intending to turn him back toward the pavilion tent. Instead she received a jolt of long-lost sensuality. She wanted to take her hand away from the searing heat, but all her energy had been sapped. She swallowed and said lamely, "They're looking for you."

"Who?" His voice seemed far away.

"The hospital people . . . the administrator."

"Oh . . ." He blinked, then looked behind her to Devlin and Hilary. "Excuse me, Lettice."

She raised her eyebrows. "I think not."

"Don't give me that damned look of yours, woman," he snapped. "Just move out of the way."

"No. And I am not giving you that damned look." She didn't move her hand, even though her control was returning. "You have something else to do, now go and do it."

"You bet your backside I do." He pulled abruptly away and began to go around her.

Lettice put herself between him and the grand-children again.

"Get out of the way, woman!"

"In a pig's eye!"

They were beginning to make a scene, and she almost didn't care. There was an excitement here, one she hadn't felt in a long, long time.

"You listen to me, Lettice Biddle," Marsh said. He looked ready to erupt as he shook his finger at her. "I am not going to allow your grandson to do to my granddaughter what you did to me."

"Give it a rest, Marsh," she said, impatient with his obtuseness. "I was nineteen and underage. Women were not allowed the freedoms they are now, if you'll remember."

His eyes narrowed. "I remember a little better

than you'd like me to. I remember an engagement less than three months later—"

"Be careful, Marsh." Lettice smiled slyly. "You'll make me think you still care."

"The hell I do!" he bellowed.

Lettice smothered her amusement at his burst of outrage. Things could be going better than she thought. "I just wanted to make sure," she said calmly.

Under the tree Hilary turned around at the sound of raised voices. One voice actually.

"I thought so," she murmured, seeing her grandfather towering over Lettice. His face was red with fury.

"What?" Devlin asked, coming out of his own reverie.

She glanced at him, but, still shaken and confused by the kiss, immediately looked away. She pointed to the makings of a grand scene behind her. "The grandparents are fighting."

He sighed. "You can dress them up, but you sure can't take them anywhere."

"I guess we'd better go put them in separate sandboxes."

"Agreed."

Despite the easy words, the tension between them was unbearable. Hilary rose to her feet before he could help her. She didn't want to feel his touch. She was afraid to. She had had a glimpse beyond the bad boy. She couldn't afford another.

He picked up his coat and stood. They walked together, side by side, leaving a good foot between them. She tried to ignore the odd pain wending its way through her at the realization that he didn't want to touch her either.

"At the rate they're going," she said, "we ought to

have them on the honeymoon before the week is out."

"Very probably." He was silent for a moment, then said, "Back there . . . that was for show, you understand."

"Absolutely," she replied, then ground her teeth together. She was getting sick of the "show."

"Children, children," Devlin said, when they reached their grandparents. "Are we having fun yet?"

"Barrels of it," Marsh snapped, but he visibly relaxed. "I was just coming to get you, Hilary, before this . . . woman put herself in my way. Can we go home now?"

"Running?" Lettice asked.

"Don't flatter yourself," Marsh said.

"I wouldn't dream of it. Besides, there's nothing to get flattered about."

"Listen, old woman—"

"Old woman!" Lettice yelped. "Old woman! Why, you old far—"

"I think we'd better get them to their corners," Hilary said to Devlin. People were looking now, recognizing that something untoward was happening.

"Round's over, Grandmother," Devlin said. He took his grandmother's arm and led her away.

Hilary did the same. Her grandfather resisted, but she tugged hard and he finally moved. He was stiff at first and muttering something under his breath about old women, but his walk eventually loosened as they made their way toward the car. To her surprise it actually became jaunty, as if he were thoroughly enjoying himself.

She turned to look back at Devlin and Lettice. Lettice seemed to be walking vigorously, like a teenager almost. She admired the long line of Devlin's back, the breadth of his shoulders, and the way his pants clung to his backside. As if he felt her gaze on him, he turned around. Hilary immediately faced forward again, humiliated at being caught.

She'd been caught by a lot of things that day, things that had left her shaken and confused and vulnerable.

Never again, she thought. Never again would Devlin Kitteridge catch her out.

Four

She couldn't believe she was doing this.

Hilary scanned the docks from the parking lot above, then cursed herself for doing so. She had had to come down to Somers Point to buy very fresh fish for the dinner she was catering. Mrs. Hargreaves was extremely fussy, after all. And Somers Point was just a hop, skip, and a jump from Wildwood.

Okay, she thought. So it was more like forty minutes in the car. A little detour on the way home. She was just taking the scenic route, she rationalized, then cursed again and admitted the truth.

She had come out of curiosity about Devlin. One couldn't help but be curious after no contact for five days. The grandparents were ripe for the striking, she had thought. He'd seemed to think so too. So why hadn't he called to arrange another act to the show?

Hilary sat back in her car seat and sighed. She'd never find the *Madeline Jo* from up here. At the hospital tea she had desperately wanted to ask whom his boat was named after, but she'd sensed a wall closing off inside him. Jealousy had curled through her then, and it had eaten at her ever since. Who was this Madeline person? And what was she to him that he'd named his boat after her? Jealousy should have been a ludicrous emotion where Devlin Kitteridge was concerned. Who the women were in his life was none of her business. She shouldn't care.

Hilary shook the thought away. Good thing this matchmaking was a joke. She had never seen two more completely incompatible people than they.

And yet that kiss . . .

She tightened her fingers around the steering wheel and forced away the sensuality curling up her thighs. It had been just a kiss and just for show. He'd said that. So had she. He might be sexy . . . Okay, he *was* sexy. He'd even been almost human the other day too. But that didn't mean she had to be stupid. Anything with Devlin was a very dead end.

Go home, she told herself. But her fingers didn't reach to switch on the ignition. Somehow they couldn't. She scanned the docks again, then gave up when she couldn't see the names on the boats. No one looked familiar either. She remembered him talking about his charters going out early in the morning. It was after one, and she wondered if he'd even be there. He could still be out, or perhaps home already, wherever that was. But if she could just get a look at the *Madeline Jo* . . .

The notion was growing ever more tempting. For some reason her mind wouldn't leave it alone. She didn't have to get up close, only close enough to know she was looking at the right one. One glimpse would do. That was all. One glimpse.

She checked her hair in the rearview mirror, made a face, then shoved her dark sunglasses back up onto her nose. She got out of the car and walked slowly to the steep ramp that led down to the docks themselves. The whole time she was looking for Devlin, ready to turn and run the moment she saw him. Curiosity was one thing, getting caught at it was another.

The sun was hot, and the cooling breezes that blew off the ocean just five blocks away were nonexistent here. The docks were busy, though, as people worked on boats or lounged on the decks. Seagulls called raucously overhead. Her heels made walking along the slatted boards a major operation in care. Her gaze was divided between watching where she was stepping and trying to spot Devlin before he spotted her. By the time she got down to where the boats were, her stomach muscles were clenched with anxiety.

She walked past small sailboats, ketches, cabin cruisers, and fishing boats with tall lookouts above the captain's cabin. She was almost to the last place on the dock before she saw it. The *Madeline Jo* was long and sleek and clearly cared for by loving hands. The boat's brass-and-chrome trim gleamed with polish, and the white paint glistened with pristine cleanliness in the bright light. Her heart dropped at the sight of the beautiful vessel.

"Veni, Vidi, Stupidi," she muttered, giving a twist to the Roman motto of "I came, I saw, I conquered." Yep, she came, she saw, she was stupid. She admitted she didn't know what she'd been expecting. A filthy, broken-down boat that signified his lack of interest in it and therefore the woman he'd named it after? She should have known what she would find after he'd talked about the boat with such pride and caring. Obviously the softer side of Devlin was reserved for another woman.

She turned around and walked back to the stairs, cursing her curiosity yet again. Satisfying the thing *could* kill a person. She took two strides up the ramp, then glanced toward the top. She froze.

Leaning against the handrail at the beginning of the ramp was Devlin. Despite the baseball cap and dark wraparound sunglasses, she knew it was he. Every bone in her body, every nerve ending, responded instantly, as if a warning siren had just started wailing.

He was gazing down at her. And he was grinning.

Hilary drew in a deep breath to regain her control, then climbed the stairs to meet her doom.

Dev had known the moment he saw her who she was. It hadn't mattered that she'd had her back to him. All his senses had come alive, and every muscle in his body had tensed at that first glance of the long line of her spine and the curve of her derriere. No woman caused that kind of reaction in him—except Hilary.

He had had to fight the urge to turn and walk away, not to let her see him. Hilary threatened him on more levels than he was prepared to fight.

And that kiss. . . .

That had scared the bejesus out of him. It had been too . . . sweet. Too damn innocent. He had gotten himself back to the safety of home and hearth without getting himself into any more trouble, and he was staying there. The grandparents could fend for themselves as far as he was concerned. Hilary was off-limits.

Until she showed up today.

He watched her hesitate at the bottom of the ramp, then climb steadily toward him. She wore another one of those prissy suits and high heels, both of which were out of place in his environment. He could feel the grin on his face, and he was helpless to stop it. He decided he'd need every bit of bravado to keep her from discovering the turmoil she created inside him.

"Fancy meeting you here," he said, when she was nearly to the top. "What happened? Did you miss me?"

She faltered for a half-step, then straightened. She stepped off the ramp, walking right past him, then turned around. "I came to see if I could get some . . . crabs."

He raised his eyebrows. "You drove all this way for crabs?"

"I need . . . fresh ingredients for a dinner I'm doing tonight."

The glasses hid her eyes. He wished he could see them, see what emotions they revealed. "Couldn't you have bought crabs live at your local market?" he asked. "Most sell them."

"They wouldn't be fresh enough," she said, shrugging. "I need them straight out of the sea."

He stared at her, oddly disappointed that she had come only for superfresh crabs. Then he shook his head. Perhaps these gourmet catering nuts would go to any extent to outdo themselves in the "fresh" department.

"Short of taking a boat out yourself, there isn't anything down here," he finally said. "Not at this time of day."

Her mouth turned downward. "Oh."

Primitive awareness shot through him at the way her lips pursed. Didn't she know she nearly killed a man when she did that?

"You could go home by way of North Wildwood," he said, dragging his gaze away from her mouth. "There're a lot of crabbers up that end of the island. They keep their traps in the water all the time."

She nodded and turned to leave. "Thank you—"

"Wait" He touched her hand. Her skin was soft, like velvet cream. Awareness frizzled along his nerve endings, seeming to suspend everything except the feel of her. He had to stop it immediately. He needed to tell her the deal was off. He brought himself under control and added, "Come down to the boat. I want to talk to you about something."

"No!"

The vehemence in her voice surprised him.

"I mean," she said quickly, "I have to get going. I have to find those crabs for tonight."

He grinned. "Lucky crabs." Then he got serious. "I'll only take a few minutes. It's important."

She glanced around. "Well, can't you say it here?"

He frowned. "I don't need a damn audience. Now, what's wrong with coming down to the boat?"

She looked around, then shrugged. "My shoes. The heels slip through the slats."

"No problem. I'll carry you."

He began to reach for her, and she immediately

backed away, somehow flipping off her high heels in the process.

"Thank you, but no," she said gravely. "I think I can manage it now."

He pointed to the wooden ramp. "You'll get splinters."

"I'll risk it."

"Okay." He waved a hand. "After you."

She walked down the ramp much less gingerly than she'd come up it. He grinned to himself. She also walked straight to his boat without stopping. His grin widened. She might have come for crabs, but she'd certainly taken a good look around while she'd been down there.

"I see you know where the 'Leakin' Lena' is," he said, as he went aboard. Looking at the mess of chum buckets and discarded tackle left from the charter, he wished he hadn't asked her down when the boat was dirty. Then he berated himself. What the hell did it matter what she might think of the *Madeline Jo*? He turned around and held out his hand. "Come aboard."

She put her shoes back on, then took his hand. It was soft and small within his own. Damn, he thought. Why did every touch seem so . . . momentous? The boat rocked slightly as she stepped down onto the deck. Once aboard, he let go of her hand, both grateful and disappointed to do so.

"Coffee? Something cold?" he asked, suddenly feeling the odd urge to play host.

She shook her head and sat stiffly on one of the low, padded benches lining the sides of the stern. He had the feeling she was ready to run at any second. She'd never struck him as the nervous type, so why was she so jumpy now?

He mentally shook himself. He had more press-

ing matters to talk about with her. He opened his
mouth to tell her that he'd thought things
through, that he figured they had accomplished
pretty much all they could with the grandparents,
that the whole damn thing was completely idiotic
anyway, so he was quitting.

"How's your grandfather?" he asked, then
clamped his jaw shut. Where had that question
come from?

"Fine, fine," she said. "He complained about
your grandmother the whole way home after we
left the tea."

"Good, good." He lapsed into awkward silence
and sat down in one of the big fishing chairs
bolted to the deck. He swiveled the seat around to
face her. She was as close to the three-step gangway as she could get. Now was the time to tell her,
he thought. Now was the moment for supreme
common sense. "Do you think he'd come out on
the boat?"

Dev actually looked around to see who'd spoken.
It couldn't have been him. Absolutely couldn't.

She shrugged, then crossed her arms tightly
around her middle, as if she were ill. "I don't know.
It's hard to say."

"Well, maybe if we got them both out in the
middle of the ocean, they'd be forced to deal with
each other."

Why was he talking about further meetings? Dev
asked himself. It was as if his common sense had
come right up to the starting gate, taken one look
at Hilary, then said, "Nope, forget it." His logic was
there; he could feel it rattling around inside him.
He just couldn't seem to get it working right.

"It's certainly worth a try," she said. He realized

she'd been silent for a few moments and wondered what she'd been thinking.

"What is?" he asked.

"Getting the grandparents on the boat."

"Oh."

His brain felt dense, sluggish. Obviously he wasn't thinking at all. He was too busy staring at her mouth. It was a perfect mouth, beautifully curved and soft, just right for kissing. He knew that.

This was insane, he thought. Women didn't get to him this way. Never. He was supposed to be calling a halt to this ridiculous scheme, and instead he was drawing himself in deeper. Hilary said nothing. She looked as unhappy as he did. She didn't like him. He knew that. Then why had she kissed him the way she had?

"Hey, Dev!"

He spun the chair in the direction of the shout. Morty Wilkins was coming in from the inlet's waterways. The man cut back the motor on his little boat, bringing it to a near stop. It drifted on the current, rocking in the wake other boats were generating.

"Who's the pretty lady?" Morty asked as Dev got up from the chair.

"None of your business," Dev said. He leaned over the starboard side to check the bow of Morty's boat. As he'd expected, it was filled with crab traps . . . and bushels of live crabs.

"Maybe," Morty said, "but she's too good for you."

Dev laughed. "She's a friend who came looking for fresh crabs. Are you willing to sell?"

"Oh, no, Dev," Hilary said, and he heard her scrambling to her feet behind him.

Morty nodded. "Sure."

Dev turned as Hilary joined him. She was shaking her head. Her body was so close to his as she leaned forward, her subtle perfume wafted around him. It overrode everything. For an instant Dev forget where he was as he drank in the scent.

"I can't impose, really."

The spell broke. Dev looked heavenward, then said, "You wanted fresh ones, and they don't get any fresher than this. How much, Morty?"

Morty stroked his chin. "Twenty bucks a half-bushel."

"I said this was a friend, not a sucker. Fifteen."

"Seventeen."

"Done. Throw me a line, Morty, and we'll divvy up."

"Really," Hilary protested. "He could get more from wherever he usually sells them. I'm sure—"

"Hand me that basket," Dev said, ignoring her.

Morty hoisted it up. Claws snapped the empty air.

"Can't get them any fresher than that," Dev repeated in satisfaction. He dumped about half into an empty bucket, then handed the basket back down to Morty. The slight pitch and roll of his boat didn't affect his balance at all.

"Thanks, Morty," he added, reaching into his pocket and pulling out some money. He passed it down. Morty grinned and restarted his motor.

Dev turned to Hilary and waved his hand. "There you go. Fresh crabs."

Hilary looked down at the bucket. "Thank you."

He frowned at her tone—it sounded almost resigned. "You don't seem happy."

She looked up and smiled. "I am. I suppose I'd better be going."

He resisted the urge to ask her to stay, knowing

it wasn't wise to be in her presence any longer. Instead he picked up the bucket before she could take it. "I'll walk you up."

When they reached her car, she opened the trunk, and he set the bucket in, wedging it against the side before closing the trunk lid. As he turned to face her, he noticed again how elegant she looked and reminded himself that she represented everything for which he had no further use. Despite his efforts to distance himself, he still seemed to have trouble remembering that. "They'll be fine in there."

She nodded as she rummaged around in her purse, then she handed over some bills. "For the crabs."

He took the money. Probably a "gentleman" wouldn't, he thought. But then he'd never claimed to be a gentleman. Besides, it was business.

"How about Sunday for the grandparents?" he asked. "Around eleven?"

She nodded again. "Sunday. Does your boat have a kitchen? I'll do lunch."

"It's a galley, and yes, it does."

She nodded a third time.

He stared at her mouth, wanting desperately to kiss her. To taste that sweetness again. That innocence. He would burst if he didn't. . . .

Panic shot through him, and he straightened. He would be a complete fool to kiss her again, and he'd been fool enough today. "Good-bye, Hilary."

"Good-bye, Devlin."

She opened the driver's door and got in. As she backed the vehicle out of the slot and drove off, she never once looked at him.

Dev shoved his hands in his jeans pockets and kicked at the gravel, completely disgusted with himself. He had no idea why he should feel disgusted, but he did. He had just committed himself to another outing with Hilary, but that wasn't the problem. He didn't know what the problem was, and he had a feeling he didn't want to.

Pushing it aside, Dev strode back to his boat.

Hours later Hilary stared into her car trunk. The crabs had made a mass escape somehow and were crawling all over the interior. Several duels were going on, and in general the creatures looked madder than wet hens. She had no idea how to get them out without losing several fingers.

It served her right for going spying, she thought. Not only had she been forced to climb onto a boat that made her heartsick, she now had twenty angry crabs she didn't want. Worse, she also had to get her grandfather to Devlin's boat on Sunday. Just what she needed, to be out on the ocean with two grandparents who were ready to kill each other . . . and Devlin.

She looked down at the crabs and shuddered.

Five

"You didn't tell me *she* would be here."

"Because I didn't know," Hilary lied. She was getting pretty good at it, she thought in resignation as she took hold of her grandfather's arm, pulling him the last few steps to the *Madeline Jo*. "You didn't have to come, you know," she added. "You were the one who insisted, remember?"

She had taken the direct route by simply telling him that she and Devlin were going out on his boat for the day. Alone. She'd extolled the joys of just the two of them isolated until her grandfather had demanded to come along. It was amazing how people responded to a little reverse psychology.

"I don't like it," Marsh grumbled, shifting the ice chest higher in front of him like a shield against the small woman standing on the deck. "She called me an old far—"

"Yes, I know," Hilary interrupted, smothering a grin.

"I think we ought to go straight home," he said.

"Go ahead. Nobody's stopping you."

"I can't . . . unless you lend me the keys to your car . . ."

She smiled. "Not a chance."

Her grandfather lapsed into a pouting silence.

"Hi, Lettice!" Hilary called out as they got within earshot.

"Ahoy!" Lettice shouted back, waving. She looked pretty in white slacks and navy-blue-and-white-striped top.

"Woman looks like a damn ad for *Sailors Weekly*," Marsh muttered.

Hilary glanced heavenward. Without divine intervention it would be a long day. Lettice's outfit looked sensible to her. So did her grandfather's polished-cotton pants and rubber-soled Rockports. Hilary wondered if her raw-silk slacks and low heels were a little inappropriate. She'd never been on a small boat before, just cruise ships and ferries. She had wanted to look her best, but now she wasn't sure if she might instead look out of place.

Devlin came up from below, and the air squeezed out of her body at the sight of him. His T-shirt and jeans were tight, outlining every muscle in his torso and thighs. He gazed at her, his blue-green eyes intense. He had the uncanny ability to make her feel he could see straight through her. He'd called her several times over the last few days, ostensibly for grandparent updates and to finalize their plans, and she had clung to the sound of his voice. Now she knew it wasn't nearly enough. She wanted the whole damn devastating package. The knowledge frightened her.

"You made it," he said, taking the ice chest from her grandfather. "It's a pleasure to see you, sir. Welcome aboard."

"Hummph!" Marsh replied, glowering at Devlin as he climbed aboard the boat. Once there, he turned his glower on Lettice.

Lettice nodded coolly in return.

Hilary sighed silently. Clearly her prayer was still on the waiting list.

Devlin held out his hand to her. She hesitated for a moment, not wanting to come on the boat. Being on it bothered her in a way she didn't like. It was as if she were jealous of the *Madeline Jo*. She shrugged the thought away, knowing it was silly. Reaching for his hand, she braced herself for the jolt of warmth his touch always engendered in her. She still wasn't prepared for it as his fingers closed around hers in a gentle, protective gesture.

"Hello," he said softly as she stepped onto the deck, then kissed her on the mouth.

She nearly staggered in her surprise. Then she realized he was back to the "show." The notion angered her for some reason. But if that was the way he wanted it, she thought, then that was what he would get.

"Hello," she purred.

His eyebrows nearly shot off his forehead.

"I think you'd better take that chest to the . . . galley," she murmured, pleased that she'd remembered the word.

He blinked. "Sure."

She glanced over at the grandparents, wondering if they should be left alone together. Her grandfather could still bolt. Both seemed to have retired to respective neutral corners, though. At least they were sitting opposite each other in the stern, both looking out in different directions. With a mental shrug she followed Devlin below, her feet slipping a little on the shiny deck. She hoped that wouldn't pose a problem.

Devlin led her through a living room area, with a table, bar, and low couches, and on to the galley. The room was the width of the boat and narrow, wide enough for only one person to maneuver around in with any ease. Two portholes were on either side of the tiny room. As she glanced out one of them, she found she noticed the rocking of the boat more down here.

He set the chest on the counter. "What the hell did you bring? This thing weighs a ton."

She frowned. "I brought everything I'd need because I didn't know what you had."

"Oh. Do you think it's safe to leave the grandparents alone?"

"If there's no blood, it'll be a major miracle," she said, shrugging. "I suppose one of us ought to referee them."

"I'll do it. I have to go up to the fly bridge anyway, to get us under way." He flipped open cabinets and doors. "This is the oven, pots and pans, dishes, refrigerator. I suppose I'd better show you how the oven works."

The oven was on the other side of him, and Hilary pressed against the wall to squeeze by him. It wasn't enough. Her breasts brushed against his chest. A red haze of sensuality instantly suffused her. Vaguely she heard a muffled sound. She wasn't sure whether it was from Devlin or from her . . . or whether she was imagining it.

"Will you hurry up?" he muttered, his cheekbones flushed with color.

His words snapped her out of the spell. Mr. Wonderful had returned, she thought wryly. The gentleness she'd seen in him at that tea and on her first visit to the boat were gone. She felt as if he'd suckered her in, lulled her into opening herself emotionally to him, and then the old Devlin showed up in triumph. Damn him, she cursed silently, and dragged herself across his torso in retaliation.

"It's so little in here, isn't it," she said, watching the color darken on his face. For a moment she thought he was going to kiss her.

Instead he did nothing, just closed his eyes.

Once she was past him, she heard his breath whoosh out of his lungs. Immediately she turned her gaze to the oven. She might have forced a response from him, but unfortunately she had one of her own to cope with. Her breasts tingled from the contact, the nipples tight buds. Blood pumped through her torso and thighs slowly, almost pulsing, her own lungs were having trouble finding air, and her stomach was fluttering. This was too dangerous, she thought.

She bent down in her cramped corner to view the oven range. The fluttering increased. Ignoring the queasy sensation, she asked, "How do you light it?"

"With a match," he snapped, twisting dials. Unseen gas hissed into the air, bringing with it the familiar rotten-eggs odor. Her insides flipped sickeningly at the smell. Devlin turned off the dials, and the hissing stopped. Her stomach returned to near normal. She swallowed and swiped at the cold beads of perspiration that had suddenly popped up on her forehead. She'd taken Dramamine early, so she knew it wasn't seasickness. It was the close quarters with Devlin.

He pointed up into the oven, to where the broiler area would be, his finger on a little hole in the front. "Light it here for both stove and oven. And don't blow us up!"

She straightened. "I'm not an idiot."

He looked her up and down. "Couldn't go by me in those shoes."

"What's wrong with my shoes?"

"Nothing a teething puppy couldn't fix."

"You," she pronounced succinctly, "have the manners of a gorilla."

"And you have the sense of an antelope! If you don't break your neck on the deck in those things, it'll be a major achievement."

He stared angrily at her, and she stared right back. The silence lasted for one interminable breathtaking minute, then they were in each other's arms, their mouths meeting in a hungry kiss. Their tongues plunged together, rubbing, curling, faster and faster. His hands were everywhere, holding her body hard against his. Excitement and hot need ran swiftly through her, and she dug her fingers into his shoulders to anchor herself against being swept away. She wanted him, and she couldn't stop herself. Not the sniping nor the logic nor their blatant incompatibility could override the combustion he produced inside her.

"Hey, you two!" Lettice shouted from above.

They broke apart instantly.

"Are we ever going to get moving?" Lettice sounded impatient.

Devlin raked his fingers through his hair, looking everywhere but at her. Hilary was grateful not to be under that intense gaze of his—especially now.

"I'd better go," he said. "You know what to do?"

She nodded, not daring to speak, for fear her voice would betray the confusion inside her.

He grunted, then turned on his heel and strode out of the galley, his shoulders filling the narrow aisle.

Hilary closed her eyes and slumped against the wall.

"Holy Christmas," she muttered, still shaken by the kiss.

Every time she lost her temper with him, she did something incredibly stupid—like stabbing him in the foot with her spoon or rubbing herself against him like a wanton.

Humiliation heated her face, and she ground her teeth together to fight the reaction. Her insides rumbled. The man was obtuse and infuriating. Never again, she thought. She'd just get herself through this outing with dignity. She hoped her grandfather would appreciate the torture she was putting herself through for him.

Her lips still tingled from it.

Dev glanced over his shoulder as they rounded the southern end of the inlet at the Crest. The grandparents were still in the stern, still staring out at the sea, still absolutely unspeaking.

At least it wasn't pistols at five paces, he thought. They'd probably blow a hole in the engine and sink the *Madeline Jo*. He'd thought he'd do anything to get his grandmother off his back, but that wasn't one of them.

He faced front again and gazed out over the water. He wished he'd drawn the line at Hilary too. Somehow she managed to push him out of control, like the way she had moved against him in the cramped galley, just the lightest touch of her body to his provoking that wild kiss. His blood heated again at the remembrance.

He scowled. Only once before had he been out of control with a woman, and the results had been tragic. A part of his brain reminded him that there was no best friend this time, that Hilary was hardly brimming over with knowledge of her own sensuality, that she wasn't a manipulator. It didn't matter. He wasn't about to lose his control again.

Still, he wondered what she might do to ignite such a kiss again. . . .

Forcing the thought of her aside, he steered the boat out away from the coast to deeper waters where schools of weakies and bluefish tended to gather. His rationale was that a bout of fishing might force the grandparents at least to acknowledge each other. Even though he wouldn't be able to hear any conversation up there in the pilothouse and over the throb of the engines, he had the distinct feeling there wasn't anything *to* hear.

That was more ominous than the two of them toe to toe, arguing at the top of their lungs.

He cut back the throttle until the boat stopped. The *Madeline Jo* bobbed up and down on the swells, rocking gently like a cradle. He climbed down the ladder.

"Why have we stopped?" Lettice asked.

"I thought we'd do a little fishing," he said, opening up the portside bench and taking out a large tackle box and two rods. "Do you fish, Marsh?"

The older man frowned, clearly not liking the use of his first name. Dev just grinned. Hell, if this worked, he'd be calling him Grandpa before too long.

"I've done some in my time," Marsh finally said.

Dev handed him the heavier rod. "This ought to do you. It's weakies and blues."

Marsh hefted the rod. "Feels right."

Dev handed the lighter one to his grandmother. He was surprised she hadn't retreated below with Hilary. But then, Lettice would be damned before she'd back down.

"And what am I supposed to do with this?" she asked.

"Fish, woman," Marsh snapped.

"Let's play nice," Dev admonished. He felt like a referee at a heavyweight fight. If he didn't stay out of the way, he was likely to get clipped.

He got the bait bucket and pierced the hooks with bits of fish. Lettice wrinkled her nose. She reminded him of the women he didn't normally allow on his boat, and the notion that his grandmother could be coquettish shocked him.

Hilary came up from below carrying a tray. He saw that her feet were bare, and he grinned. She'd probably had enough of slipping and sliding around the galley.

"I was missing you," he said, falling easily into his role of lover. He refused to admit he fell into it a little too easily.

Her lips turned up in a weak smile. "I missed you too. I've made iced tea with mint."

Lettice instantly put down her rod and took a glass.

Marsh glanced at it disparagingly. "None for me."

"I've got the cheap stuff out of the jar just for you," Hilary said.

Her grandfather grinned at her, then fed out his line. Dev frowned at the obvious private joke. He hated private jokes.

"What happened to your shoes, child?" Lettice asked.

Hilary's face turned from pale to red. "I forgot them."

"Let her be," Marsh said, looking out over the water.

"I was only asking," Lettice said sharply.

Dev looked at Hilary, then glanced heavenward. He took the tray from her and set it on the bench. "Come up with me."

"I have lunch . . ." she began.

"For a little while," he wheedled. Out of the corner of his eye he saw Marsh grimace. It disappointed him that Hilary's grandfather didn't like him, though he didn't know why he should care.

Snorting at his own craziness, he put his hand on the small of Hilary's back to guide her toward the steps to the fly bridge. His fingers fit perfectly along the curve of her spine.

He let her climb first, taking pleasure in the view of her rounded derriere. She was one of the few women he'd ever seen who looked good in pants. In a pair of tight jeans she'd be a knockout. He doubted, though, that she even owned a pair. He sighed. What a waste.

Once up in the fly bridge, Hilary leaned against the far window, her bottom braced on the tiny ledge. She yawned, then looked down at her feet.

Dev started up the motor again and pushed the throttle forward slightly so that the boat moved slowly through the water.

"Where are we going?" she asked.

"In circles," he answered. "We're trolling while those two fish. I just hope they don't try to use each other as bait."

"Have they been sniping again?"

He glanced at her, then went back to concentrating on steering the boat in circles. "They haven't been saying anything at all. They've been sitting there like two icebergs. That's why I got the fishing gear out. If they're not going to talk to each other, at least they can be catching my dinner. I figure it'll keep them from killing each other too."

"Well, let's take hope in the fact that my grandfather didn't take a hike when—"

"He can't out in the middle of the ocean," Dev broke in, grinning. "That was the whole point."

"No, on the dock before we left. I thought he would when he spotted your grandmother."

"Did he ever tell you what happened between them?"

She shook her head. "I only know he blames your grandmother completely. I have the impression she dumped him—maybe for your grandfather?"

"Come on," he said. "My grandmother can be a pain, but she's not a tease or anything. She's honest. Sometimes too honest, but she's honest."

"I wasn't implying that she wasn't," Hilary said.

Her tone was touchy. Dev decided one fighting couple was enough and changed the subject to something innocuous. "What's for lunch?"

"Wild mushrooms in black ravioli with crab sauce."

He looked at her. "You're kidding. For lunch?"

"Yes." She leaned her head back against the glass and closed her eyes. He had a tantalizing view of her throat.

"What the hell are black ravioli anyway?" he asked. "Burnt to a crisp?"

"It's a form of pasta, very dark from the spices and black walnuts in the flour mix."

"Sounds . . . Never mind. What else are we having?"

"Lobster salad à la Saigon." There was a long silence. He was about to ask what that was, when she moaned slightly and added, "It's lobster chunks with big basil leaves and a vinegar-based dressing. Blueberry-carrot cake with cream cheese frosting for dessert."

"Have they caught anything back there yet?" he asked hopefully.

"I . . . no." She made a funny sound, and he glanced over at her. Her head was still back, her eyes still closed. Her skin was almost translucent, like fine pearls. She yawned. A vague alarm bell went off in his head as he wondered why she seemed so tired. Probably from cooking all that strange food, he decided.

"I'd better go check on lunch," she said, abruptly raising her head and opening her eyes.

She immediately looked away from him and headed toward the steps, lurching a little from the boat's rocking. She disappeared down the steps faster than he'd thought she could in bare feet.

Dev knew an excuse when he heard it. Dammit, he thought. She mystified him, making easy small talk with him one moment, then leaping away the next as if he had a contagious disease. She didn't have to make her intolerance of him that clear. He'd gotten the hint long ago.

On the other hand, he added, though she might not tolerate him on one level, on another she'd damn near kissed his socks off. Dev grinned. There was more to the coolly social butterfly than was on the surface. She probably didn't like the way she responded to him. As a matter of fact, he bet it irritated the hell out of her. Maybe he ought to "irritate" her some more.

A voice inside him reminded him that she "irritated" him. And she did it very well.

The silence was deafening.

Marsh was very good at fishing, Lettice thought as she waved her rod back and forth.

"That won't get a fish," he said, his voice cold.

She knew that, but she preferred for him to think she was a novice. If he had to help her, then he had to talk. . . .

Stopping her movement, she said, "Really? I thought you had to sort of jerk the line so that the fish sees it."

"Not in deep-sea fishing. The waves mask the movement. That's why Dev's keeping the boat going. Trolling it's called, to entice the fish. He's doing a damn good job too." This last was said with reluctant admiration.

Lettice suppressed a smile as she wondered if he realized he was having a conversation with her. She wasn't about to tell him. The children had come up with quite a scheme in this outing, a euphemism, she was sure, for stranding her and Marsh in the middle of the ocean. She was proud of them too. Unfortunately Marsh was a bigger holdout than she'd thought. But she had time. . . .

No, she didn't, she reminded herself. She'd already wasted sixty years.

Suddenly she felt a tug on her line, then a pull. A hard pull. "I've got something!" she shouted.

"Reel it in steady and don't wave the line about!" Marsh said excitedly.

"I know—" Lettice stopped herself. "What do I do, Marsh?"

He jumped up from his chair and was over to hers in two strides, his own line forgotten. "Just what I said. Reel it in steady. You've probably got yourself a blue."

She turned the spindle and knew instinctively from the amount of resistance that she had more than a bluefish. Surreptitiously she let go of the spindle, and the line spun out.

"Oh!" she said helplessly.

"Here." Marsh put his arm around her, his hand covering hers and placing it back on the spindle to stop it. "Just reel it in, Lettice."

She settled in for the duration, content.

Hilary stared down at the shiny-black pasta in the long glass dish, and her stomach heaved over.

She raced for the small porthole and flung it open, breathing in deeply to clear her head. Unfortunately all she breathed in was the smell of rank salt and diesel. She slammed the porthole shut, then wet a paper towel, covering her face with the cool, damp material and pressing her fingers against her lips. She hadn't been able to stand talking about food any longer, so she'd fled the deck with Devlin. But this was worse. Much worse.

It must be the flu, she thought. She felt clammy and feverish at the same time. She got the Dramamine packet out of her purse and read the directions—or tried to. They swam before her eyes. She yawned again and wondered why she couldn't seem to stop those yawns. Worse, she could actually feel the boat going around and around and around. Couldn't Devlin just park the damn thing? Butterflies fluttered another warning.

She decided it was long past time for another pill. If it was the flu, it ought to help her stomach and dizzy head. And if it wasn't, the Dramamine ought to cure her.

She drank the pill down with water and was instantly sorry when her gut roared out an immediate protest.

She leaned her face against the cool wall and closed her eyes. She wasn't going to make it through this lunch, she thought. She was ill. Unbidden, she remembered when she'd been deathly ill with the flu once before and had hid it long enough to cater a dinner party for twenty-five. Her client was still talking about how wonderful the food and ambience had been. In fact she was her best client now. Considering it, Hilary decided she'd felt just as bad then. Worse. Really ill. Ready to make the bathroom her best friend.

Maybe she ought to take another Dramamine, just to be sure.

Common sense told her to wait, but five minutes later the combined smells of crab sauce, cooked mushrooms, and vinegar had her shaking out another pill and washing it down with a minimum of water. She nearly didn't survive the second dose.

Make it stop, make it stop, her brain chanted as she slid down the wall to sit on the floor. Shaking, she forced herself to crawl into the other room to get away from the smell. The first thing that swam into view was the low, padded bench that masqueraded as a sofa. She crawled up onto it and curled into a ball, closing her eyes. The sofa spun and rocked, but she was beyond caring. She was going to die.

Death by ravioli, she thought. It would be a fitting ending for someone in her profession.

She only hoped she didn't throw up first.

Dev pulled back on the throttle, stopping the boat, then climbed down onto the deck to watch Marsh help his grandmother reel in her catch. Progress was in the making, he thought. He'd better go tell Hilary. Besides, he was hungry enough to eat black ravioli and lobsters from Vietnam, or whatever the hell it was called.

He went below and stopped dead on the bottom rung. Hilary was lying on the saloon sofa, her knees against her chest. She looked lifeless.

"Hilary, what's wrong?" he asked, crossing the room.

She didn't answer. He pressed his hand against her forehead. It was cool, but clammy. Her skin was so pale, paler than when she'd been on deck. Almost a pallor, he decided.

"Hilary!" he said loudly.

"Sick," she mumbled. "Flu."

Everything clicked in his head, and he said, "You don't have the flu. You're seasick."

She groaned. "No . . . took Dramamine."

"Wonderful." He looked around the room for help, then remembered his grandmother. He turned and went back up on deck.

"Hilary's seasick!" he announced.

Marsh glanced at him. "Get her to the bathroom."

"No, I mean she's lying on the sofa looking half-dead."

"Best place for her," his grandmother said. "Just put a bucket beside her, in case she gets sick again. Oh, Marsh, it's really pulling. I don't think—"

"Of course you can," Marsh said, helping her turn the spindle.

"What about Hilary?" Dev asked.

"Let her sleep," both grandparents said.

"What about lunch?"

"Eat it," Marsh said.

"Save some for us," Lettice said. "We'll be hungry once we get this in."

"Lettice, I think you've got a shark! Play him!"

Dev stomped below. Damn lot of good they were, he thought. Once they caught the fish, he'd head back to shore. Hilary would be better then.

He got a blanket and covered her with it, then stared at her, wondering what else he could do. They'd been at sea for less than two hours, and she was completely seasick. He lived by the sea. He loved it. If he'd ever needed proof that they were incompatible, he'd just gotten it.

Why hadn't she told him she got seasick? Hadn't she realized it could happen? He remembered her saying something about Dramamine. Had she taken some? Didn't she know she had to take it *before* she came on board? What a day. He had two septuagenarians playing Captain Ahab up on deck and one half-dead woman in the saloon.

He shook his head, annoyed with himself. He was the one who'd had this brilliant idea in the first place. If he'd just ignored his grandmother's parade of women, he would be happily content with his life. A little, perverse voice told him, *Not happy and not content.*

Cursing under his breath, he went into the galley. Somehow Hilary had managed to get everything cooked and set out in pretty dishes. One look at the gleaming black pasta and he knew instantly why she was so sick. Black pasta was enough to flip anyone's nose up. Still, it smelled good. The salad looked good, too, with its chunks of meaty lobster and big basil leaves.

He got a fork out of the drawer and tried the pasta. It was a little on the cool side, but the flavors burst in his mouth like exquisite ambrosia. A bite of the salad told him it was outstanding. He ate some more of both, straight out of the dishes.

Hilary's job might be a froufrou, but, boy, could she cook.

Six

Hilary slowly surfaced from a black sleep. Her tongue felt woolly, her mouth had a bad taste to it, her head was pounding, and her stomach felt queasy. Slowly she blinked, then raised her eyelids.

She was in a strange room that seemed to be rocking gently like a cradle. A rough blanket covered her. Underneath she was nearly naked except for a T-shirt and her underwear.

"Ah, she wakes," Devlin said, coming down some steps on the other side of the room. "About damn time."

"Where am I?" she asked, instinctively clutching the blanket closer to her as she sat up.

"The *Madeline Jo*," he said. "My boat."

Everything came back in a rush. "Where's my grandfather and Lettice?"

"Back home beginning their *Monday*."

"Monday?" she squeaked, horrified. "It's Monday?"

What happened, she wondered, to Sunday afternoon, Sunday evening . . . and Sunday night?

She glanced down at the blanket covering her in shock, then looked back up at Devlin. He was dressed in jeans and a short-sleeve knit top. She swallowed convulsively and asked, "What—what happened to my clothes?"

"You don't remember a thing, do you?" he asked in return.

She shook her head. "No . . . I . . . no."

"Well-l," he said, drawing out the word as he sat down on the edge of the sofa. She scooted back against the wall. "You were something, Hilary. Full of surprises—"

"I slept with you?" she asked in a panic. "I couldn't have—"

"Clearly a fate worse than death," he said, wryly.

"I'm sure it was fine," she added, not wanting to hurt him. "I mean, I'm positive you were . . . we were . . ." She stopped. "What were we?"

"Not that."

She sighed in relief. He snorted and got up from the sofa.

"Then how did I . . ." she began tentatively.

"You were sick," he snapped. "*Very* sick. And the damn grandparents refused to take you home. Your grandfather didn't even put up too much of a fuss about leaving you. 'She's too sick,'" he mimicked in a high, sarcastic voice. "'She'll have to stay.' You were only lying on the sofa, nearly dead. You should have been tossing your cookies when you were halfway to Philadelphia. Instead you tossed them here on my boat. Lucky me."

She groaned, half from embarrassment, half from the mention of the dirty deed. The worst part was she couldn't remember a thing.

"You're not getting sick again, are you?" he asked in terror.

She shook her head. "No. I'm sorry, Devlin."

"Why the hell didn't you tell me you were sick?" he demanded. "Why the hell didn't you say you got seasick? We never would have gone out. I had to cancel the charter for this morning because of this. Do you have any idea what it's like to face four guys at five-thirty in the morning and tell them to turn around and go home?"

"I'll pay you," she said quickly.

"I don't want your damn money!" he roared.

She pressed her hands over her ears and shuddered. Why did he have to yell?

In a quieter voice he said, "Since you insisted on being so idiotic, why didn't you take something before you came on the boat so that you wouldn't get sick in the first place?"

"I did," she said, holding her head. It ached from his lecture. She couldn't seem to find the words to shut him up.

Something landed on the cushions next to her. It was a large bowl.

"Use it," he snapped.

"I'm not sick," she said, raising her head. "Just mortified, okay? Look, I'm sorry I was such a disaster, but the medicine worked before on the cruise ship, and I don't understand why it didn't work this time. I even took three—"

"You took three!" He stared at her. "You were lucky you didn't kill yourself."

"I didn't take them all at once, you cluck," she said, furious with him for making her sound like a stupid person. "Just the last two, to stop the sickness *before* I got sick."

He looked her up and down. "It didn't work."

Delayed realization finally set in. She was in

different clothes because he'd undressed her. He'd actually taken her clothes off and put a T-shirt on her while she'd been . . . All of her had been exposed to his view. Devlin Kitteridge's view. Her rose lace-and-silk panties didn't hide much. No, they hid nothing, she was positive of it. Of all the men to see her like that. She felt oddly violated and aroused at the same time.

Her humiliation rose one hundred percent at the notion. She wouldn't show it, she thought, determined to hold on to whatever dignity she had left.

"If you'll give me my clothes, I'll be on my way," she said, raising her chin.

"You don't want them." He grinned. "I have to admit that for all my annoyance at losing a charter, it was interesting to see you be human."

"How lovely," she said. "Please give me my clothes."

"I dumped them overboard."

Her jaw dropped in astonishment. "You dumped them?"

He nodded, raising his eyebrows as if she'd asked a ridiculous question.

"Why couldn't you have washed them?"

"Do you see a washing machine?"

She looked around. "No, but—"

"Believe me, you wouldn't have wanted them. I'll lend you a pair of my jeans."

"No, thank you," she said primly. The last thing she wanted was to be in any more of his clothes.

His eyes narrowed. "You intend to walk up the dock in that blanket?" He relaxed his fanny back against the wall, his arms crossed. "This I gotta see."

She was no fool. "I will take a pair of jeans."

He shook his head. "Hilary, Hilary, Hilary. You

made a decision, and far be it from me to allow you to back out now. You don't want to be wishy-washy, do you?"

She leaned her head back and closed her eyes. "Heaven forbid."

He would make her do it, she thought. It was just the kind of perverse thing he liked. She'd never met a man who was so full of contradictions as Devlin.

Something landed against her again, clinking against the bowl. She opened her eyes to find a pair of jeans on the sofa.

"I'm not a total ogre," he said.

She smiled. "No, you're not. Just first runner-up."

Her words forced a reluctant smile from him. "Get dressed, and then we'll get something to eat and take you home."

She wasn't sure if she was ready for food, but she'd kill for a cup of tea.

She reached out and picked up the jeans, intending to find the nearest bathroom. Instead the feel of the soft denim instantly brought to mind the image of his body inside those jeans, his skin touching everywhere. In a few minutes *her* body would be inside them, her skin touching everywhere, the most intimate part of her against where the most intimate part of him . . .

A low moan rose from the back of her throat. She could feel beads of sweat on her forehead that had nothing to do with seasickness.

"Are you sick again?"

His questions dissipated her sensual awareness. She drew in a deep breath to steady herself, her fingers tightening around the jeans.

"No," she said, and knew it was another lie.

She was sick, sick at heart. She doubted there was a cure.

When Hilary finally emerged from the head, Dev couldn't help staring at her. His jeans fit tightly around her calves and thighs. She looked just as fabulous as he'd thought she would. And every time he wore those jeans, he'd remember.

Fortunately his black T-shirt was too large for her frame, but unfortunately, he realized as he continued staring, it did nothing to hide the curves of her breasts. She crossed her arms over her chest to compensate for her missing bra. It didn't help. He knew all too well her bra was down in Neptune's closet. He'd heaved the thing over the side himself. In fact it had given him great pleasure to throw all of those prissy clothes overboard for more than the obvious reason.

But now . . . she looked so different. Gone was the social butterfly. Barefoot, with her hair down around her shoulders and brushed shiny, she had metamorphosed into any earthy, sexy, incredibly approachable woman. Yet the elegance was still there, an integral part of her, the part that somehow held the most allure.

She smiled almost shyly, but didn't step any closer. "I never asked, but how did it go yesterday? With the grandparents."

"They caught a shark," he said, his voice surprisingly hoarse. He cleared his throat and found more words. "A four-foot blue, a baby. They threw it back."

"Together?" she asked, incredulous.

"Yep. They were talking too." A part of him wished they hadn't. It would mean no more outings with Hilary. To dispel the disturbing thought, he turned back to the stove and the breakfast. "If the truce lasted through the car ride home, it would be a miracle."

"I assume they took Lettice's car?"

"You assume wrong. My grandmother is barred by the family from driving. They took yours. Eggs and toast are ready."

"They took mine!" she squawked. "Now how am I supposed to get home?"

He grinned at her. "Me. Now, take a plate and eat."

She did and whirled back into the other room. Dev followed happily. There was something to be said for being behind a woman as she walked. It made a man want to run his hands down the length of her long spine and find the curves of her derriere. From there imagination went rampant.

He drank coffee while she ate, at first tentatively, then with gusto. "It's not as good as what you could do," he said.

"It's terrific," she mumbled around bites.

"Where did you learn to cook like you do?"

"I was a sous-chef at the White Dog Café in Philadelphia," she replied. "A friend of mine owns it, and she let me train there. I worked for a couple of other restaurants but got tired of it and went out on my own." She paused, then added with a little smile, "Into the froufrou catering business."

"If yesterday's lunch was anything to go by, you give one hell of a froufrou."

She chuckled. "I take it lunch did come off, then."

"Actually I ate most of it. The grandparents were too busy catching fish, although they did eat later. You had it all ready except for being on the table."

"At least Mr. Savarin won't be turning over in his grave that I was derelict in my duty."

He frowned. "What does a coffee manufacturer have to do with your being a cook?"

"Brilliant Savarin was one of the greatest master chefs of all time," she told him.

"Makes one helluva cup of coffee too."

She giggled, then grew serious. "I really have made a mess of your day. What can I do to make it up to you?"

When she asked him like that, in a voice that could melt a man's insides, he was ready to give *her* anything, rather than the other way around.

"Nothing," he said, watching her eyes. "I don't want anything from you."

He saw her hurt, then she shuttered her eyes.

" I see," she said.

But she didn't see, he thought. She didn't see at all how she could twist him up.

It wasn't something he planned to tell her either.

The afternoon was just beginning when he finally drove up to her town house.

The tension had reappeared during the long car ride, and Hilary had had no idea how to stop it. Just sitting next to Devlin had produced an awareness that grew as the miles did. Every line of his body, every movement of his, had set off a deep pulsing within her. The air couldn't seem to find her lungs, no matter how deeply she breathed it in. Hot, heavy syrup seemed to have replaced her blood, especially deep in her pelvis, where it throbbed convulsively. The car's air-conditioning didn't cool her off. Instead she felt as if the August heat and humidity had built to an all-time high inside her. Even telling herself that she'd humiliated herself in front of him—albeit unwittingly—didn't stop the awareness and underlying physical tension.

She didn't attempt conversation. Halfway up from the shore it had died an uncomfortable death anyway. Devlin had turned the radio on. He stared out the windshield, watching traffic, and she stared out the side window, watching the sights.

"Thank you," she said, when he pulled into a parking slot near her town house.

"Yeah," he muttered, turning off the ignition. "I see your car made it home all right."

She turned around to look at her regular parking spot, but Devlin was in the way. A tiny voice inside her told her to stop staring. She could, she thought, if he stopped staring at her first. But those blue-green eyes held her mesmerized. She could feel her nipples tighten, and she could see his awareness of her reaction in his quickened breathing.

He reached across the space between them until his fingers touched her hair. They threaded through the strands slowly, as if testing them against his skin.

"Do you know you never wear it free like this?" he said in a quiet voice.

"Yes, I do," she said, surprised that her calm tone betrayed none of the wild confusion bursting inside of her.

"I've never seen it."

"Oh." She knew she had to get out of the car now. "I should go." She didn't move.

"Yes. Yes, you should," he said, even as his hand cupped her cheek.

The space between them suddenly closed to nothing. Their mouths met instantly, hungrily, in a thorough, breath-stealing kiss that inflamed her. His arm came around her, pulling her to him until her breasts were pressed to his chest. Only thin cotton separated flesh from flesh, and it proved to be no barrier at all. His fingers wrapped around her hair. His tongue circled and rubbed against hers, provoking the maddening sensations to even greater heights.

Warmth trickled along her flesh. She gripped his upper arm, her fingers curling around the corded muscles. It was as if she had anchored herself to him, rooting herself in reality even as she was being swept away. His fingers left her hair to trace a path down her cheek, then down between their bodies until he found her breast.

She moaned as his thumb rubbed across her nipple, fanning the aching heat to a fever pitch. She had wanted him to touch her like this, but the satisfaction soared the wanting to another level. She wanted him, needed him. Now.

She was so hot . . . unbearably hot . . . intolerably . . .

Another kind of reality penetrated. Hilary realized she was in a car, in front of any of her neighbors who cared to see, necking with Devlin. More than necking. Damn near down in the front seat and ready to make the car rock.

She pulled away, panting for breath. With the engine off, the air-conditioning was off, and the heat had built quickly. She was nuts, she thought, horrified that she was kissing a man uncontrollably in broad daylight. And he was touching her, in public. Idiotic . . . crazy . . . What had happened to her brain? All her common sense seemed to fly out the window when it came to Devlin Kitteridge.

"Thanks again," she mumbled, whipping open the car door and scrambling out of the passenger seat. The air outside seemed chilly compared with the heat they'd generated in the car.

She slammed the door shut behind her and half-ran to her front door. She heard his engine start and his car screech out of the parking lot.

She didn't look back as she fumbled with the door lock. Finally the key went in straight, and she was inside in a flash. She leaned back against the steel door, desperate to barricade herself in, away from that man.

A little voice inside her told her it was too late.

Way too late.

Dev slammed on the brakes right in front of his grandmother's door. As he strode toward the house, the door opened. His grandmother stood on the threshold.

"I came for lunch," he said, not breaking his stride.

"Is Hilary okay now?" Lettice asked.

"Yes."

"Did she slam the door in your face again?"

"No."

He walked past her into the house. The knick-knacks and the tables in the foyer hadn't changed from his youth. Even the Ming vase still sat atop the delicate Hepplewhite table, seasonal flowers blooming brightly in contrast to the muted Chinese porcelain. Once he had come joyously to this home, basking in his family's no-nonsense affection and security. Then he had hated to come, hated to face his memories.

For once, though, the past didn't come rushing at him, threatening to overwhelm him. In fact it didn't come at all. His mind was too filled with that kiss.

He was getting in too deep, he thought. Much too deep.

With a woman like Hilary, a man might never surface again.

Seven

He hated dinner parties.

Dev tugged at his restricting collar, the alien tie feeling, as always, like a noose around his neck.

"Stop fidgeting," his grandmother admonished him as she knocked on the door.

"I'm not fidgeting," he grumbled, twitching his shoulders against the tight fabric of his suit jacket.

"You look like Salome doing the dance of the seven veils," Lettice said.

He almost snapped back that she wasn't all that calm, cool, and collected herself. He'd sensed a new tension in her these past several days, but she had said nothing about Marsh, the boat, or the ride home.

Dev wanted to ask, but decided against it.

The front door opened, and Lettice instantly turned on the Kitteridge charm. She swept inside and kissed the cheeks of the hostess and host. "Margo, Richard. How lovely. You remember my grandson, Devlin? Of course you do, Richard. You were both in school together."

Dev smiled and shook hands with the tall, fair-haired man. "Last time I saw you, you were skinny and nearsighted."

Richard chuckled. "And you were trouble."

"He still is," Lettice said.

"Thank you for having me," Dev said to his hostess, shaking her offered hand.

"Oh, no, Devlin. I am just thrilled you chose my little soiree to come out of . . . retirement." Margo giggled, clearly overjoyed to have the biggest gossip coup of the year.

Dev just smiled at her and walked on into the room, wishing he hadn't come and wondering why he had. But he knew the answer, and her name was Hilary. Lettice had mentioned at lunch the other day that she would be here. He'd snatched up the vague offer, trading on his old acquaintance with Richard to get his grandmother to make a major faux pas and ask to bring her own guest. He'd even promised to be on his best behavior.

As he looked around for Hilary, he admitted he should have left things alone, especially after what had happened in his car. Hilary rattled cage doors long shut tight. But he'd no sooner heard her name than he'd leaped right back in.

Now, he told himself, he needed to see her on neutral territory, to explain . . . something. He wasn't sure what he was supposed to explain, but the urge was riding him too much to be ignored.

The front room was enormous and filled with people. Obviously Richard had done all right for himself. At least he hadn't lost whatever he'd inherited.

"Thanks, but no thanks," Dev muttered, thinking of himself. Everyone was dressed formally too. At least he had on a tie.

"What did you say?" Lettice asked.

He shook his head.

"Well, see you behave yourself. I'm trying to get Richard to be a sponsor at the next Villanova Hospital Ball, and I do not want you to blow it for me. Or you will regret it," she added in an ominously quiet tone.

"Yes, Grandmother. And by the way, there'll be hell to pay on your end if Hilary doesn't show up. And I don't see her."

"Oh, she's here, otherwise Margo would be foaming at the mouth. Devlin, dear, there's something you need to understand—"

"I thought so!" a voice interrupted. "Devlin Kitteridge."

Dev turned to find another old acquaintance bearing down on him, saying, "I haven't seen you since that . . . See, everyone, I told you it wasn't Miles."

He gritted his teeth as he was pulled into a large knot of people. After initial greetings the men were blatantly uninterested in him because he no longer had any power in business or in their society. The women were more predatory, and all of them seemed to be clones of his hostess. Maybe he'd walked into a remake of *The Stepford Wives*, he mused. Everyone talked out of squared jaws, and the cultured tones grated on his nerves.

He knew the women were gathering around him only because of his value as gossip. If he had to endure much of this, he'd be a babbling idiot. Where *was* Hilary?

"But I wanted the quail! I asked for the quail! I cannot believe you *didn't bring it!*"

Margo's loud, angry voice overrode every conversation in the room. Dev turned and was stunned to see that Hilary was the recipient of Margo's words. The two women were standing on the threshold of the dining room. Hilary was dressed in a long dark skirt and blouse. Dev noted that the subdued colors did nothing to hide her fabulous curves.

"I am sorry, Margo," Hilary said, somehow not losing a shred of her poise despite being screamed at. "As I explained to you, the dish presented certain problems—"

"Well, you've completely ruined my dinner!" the woman exclaimed. "I certainly don't think I should be charged when the fault is yours."

"Of course," Hilary said, nodding graciously. "I think you will be pleased with the Breaded Rack of Lamb I've substituted, however."

"I doubt that," the woman snapped. "But I suppose it'll have to do."

Hilary tilted her head in acquiescence, then vanished into the dining room. Dev blinked. The incident had happened so fast, he and everyone else were still gaping.

Immediately he strode away from the group surrounding him, heading for Hilary. He hated the way she'd just been treated and the way everyone had looked down on her. He'd discovered long ago that the social niceties were a relative thing. As he passed his hostess, who was smirking in triumph, he muttered, "Get some manners, lady."

Margo gasped, and satisfaction ran through him. Behind him he heard his grandmother say, "Hilary's Rack of Lamb is absolutely terrific. She doesn't make it for everyone, you know. Margo, she hasn't ruined your dinner. She's just *made* it. . . ."

Dev grinned as he entered the dining room. Lettice was blowing her perspective sponsor without any help from him. It was at moments like this when he actually liked his grandmother. Stopping by the huge dining table to look around, he saw Hilary disappearing through a door at the far end of the room. The door hadn't yet closed behind her when he caught the handle and stepped into a brightly lit kitchen.

The room was in chaos, with pots, pans, dishes, glasses, chopping boards, and food covering every inch of the counters. Two people he didn't know seemed to be banging things everywhere, and riding over the top of it all was a steady stream of curses coming from Hilary.

"You are human," Dev breathed, as she spouted the seven words one couldn't say on television in rapid-fire succession.

She turned at the sound of his voice, and his eyes widened in amazement. She looked harried and flushed, all the poise momentarily gone.

"What are you doing here, Devlin?" she finally asked, then immediately said, "Go away. The waiters didn't show up tonight, that stupid excuse for a woman is out there losing me every potential customer in the place and a few old ones, too, I'd wager, besides screwing me out of my fee. Damnit, I told that cheapskate we couldn't do twenty-six quails in wild-elderberry sauce because her kitchen couldn't handle it."

"You could punch Margo's lights out," Dev said. "I'll back you." He knew Hilary would never do it.

"Miss Manners wouldn't approve," she said, confirming his opinion. "Dev, please go away. I don't have time to deal with you."

"Grandmother is talking you up like you're the best thing since that coffee guy. And if you're shorthanded, I have two of them." He held them up. "They're yours. Just tell me where to put them."

Before Hilary could speak, the other woman in the kitchen did. "Put chocolate-syrup stripes on those plates over there, run a knife down them every inch or so, and plop a slice of that cake on it. Then put them in the fridge . . . somewhere." The woman had short red hair and never once looked up from her stirring of something in a pot on the stove. The third person was a young man in his twenties who had the same coloring and build as the woman.

"Jane, this is a guest," Hilary said.

"And this is no time to be choosy."

"Right," Hilary said. "Dev, get over there and stripe those plates. Jeremy, you get the greens ready for the tournedos in salad. I'll gratin the oysters. Jane can't leave the risotto. We'll never do that dish again."

"You got that right," Jane said, one hand still constantly stirring while every so often the other poured dollops of liquid from a bowl into the pot. "My arm is killing me."

Dev shed his jacket and threw himself into the madhouse. He wasn't sure how many stripes he was supposed to put on the plates, but decided they didn't need an amateur asking questions every two seconds.

"I'll be damned," he said as he ran a butter knife in a straight line across the stripes and discovered it created an elegant pattern on the plate. "Hey! Look at this!"

Hilary glanced up from her oysters and grinned. "Pretty."

As he continued to rapidly stripe plates, the madhouse eventually sorted itself into a state of controlled chaos. Clearly Jane and Jeremy were the main chefs, and it seemed from the conversation that they had an investment in the business. But the three of them working together spoke of mutual respect and friendship. Dev hadn't realized Hilary had friends. Seeing her work harder at her job than he did at his own also made him realize how unfair his froufrou comments had been. He'd been unfair to Hilary on several fronts, it seemed.

The work became more intense as everyone rushed to bring the various elements of the dinner together at the same moment. The three professionals formed an assembly line and arranged the appetizer, transforming china and shells into a work of art. The kitchen was a large one for a home, but a cramped hole-in-the-wall when it came to cooking for twenty-six. Finished appetizer plates sat on every available flat space except the floor.

Margo came in once to check on the meal. Dev glared at her, and she looked as if she'd swallowed her tongue. At least she made no remarks on finding him in the kitchen. She didn't harass Hilary again either.

"Jeremy, you and I will serve," Hilary said when the appetizers were done. She smoothed her hair into place while Jeremy unwrapped his apron and rolled down his sleeves. Both were transformed into efficient maître d' and waiter. Looking at her,

Dev still couldn't quite believe he'd heard her saying things forbidden on the docks.

She turned to him. "Devlin, you'd better stop now so that you can get ready for dinner—"

"Hell, no. I've got plates to fancy up," he said.

"Besides, I need him for the main course," Jane added.

"See, I'm actually wanted."

"Devlin." She rubbed her hand across her forehead in clear frustration. "I'm grateful for your help, but clients take a dim view of guests working in the kitchen during their parties. You'll lose them for me."

"Tell them I went home sick."

She gaped at him in horror. "They'll blame the food! Besides, Margo knows you're in here."

"You'll never have her as a client again anyway," he said. At her still-stubborn look, he added, "Tell them I'm training with you. Or watching the operation from the inside because I'm thinking of investing in it."

"Not bad for an excuse," Jeremy broke in.

"It's every faux pas in the book," Hilary said.

"Fauxing a pas here and there is good for the soul," Dev said. "And if you don't get out there with the food, everyone's going to be in here fauxing their pas all over the place just to eat."

Hilary laughed, giving up the fight. Picking up four appetizer plates, she swept into the dining room, with Jeremy right behind her.

"How does she do it?" Dev asked, finally giving vent to his admiration of her as he joined Jane at the assembly line.

"Great brains and great calm," the woman said. She pointed to a silver platter. "Hold that while I slide the lamb onto it.

As he did, she expertly lifted two decorated racks of lambs onto the serving platter. They smelled like ambrosia. Dev wondered if Hilary could do for sex what she did for catering, for if she did, she'd be tremendous in bed. The thought was enticing. One thing puzzled him, though.

"Why go to all this trouble if you're not getting the fee?" he asked. "Why not walk away from the job? Especially after the crap Margo dished out."

"Because there are customers here tonight, old ones and still a chance for new ones if we pull the dinner off," Jane answered. "How we handle a screwup can actually make more brownie points with people than a meal that comes off perfectly. Besides, we'd get a bad reputation for nonperformance if we didn't."

It made sense to him. "Have you been with Hilary long?"

"Since the beginning. My brother and I got tired of working for overrated chefs about the same time Hilary did. We went in together with her, using her contacts on the Main Line to get us clients." She grinned. "We did a half-million dollars worth of business last year."

Dev whistled. He had *a lot* to apologize for.

Hilary rushed back into the kitchen, Jeremy again on her heels.

"If your grandmother raves anymore," she said, "I'll be catering the White House next. But everyone looks pleased, except Margo." She grabbed four more plates, and was gone in an instant, Jeremy behind her like a shadow.

Dev closed his mouth, realizing his chance to speak with her was already lost.

"She likes you," Jane said.

He made a face. "How can you tell?"

"She didn't kick you out on your butt."

"Hilary would never do that," he said, shaking his head. He couldn't imagine it.

Jane snorted. "You don't know Hilary."

Dev recognized a hard truth when he heard it. He didn't know Hilary. He hadn't wanted to. In fact he'd gone out of his way to keep from knowing anything about her. And what he had thought he'd known was turning out to be all wrong.

"Now what?" he asked when they finished with the main course.

"Wash dishes."

"Wash dishes?"

Jane grinned. "Wash dishes."

Dev decided that next time an escape was offered he'd take it.

Hilary cleared the last of the dessert plates from the table, walked into the kitchen, and collapsed into the nearest chair. After a moment she noticed that Devlin was up to his elbows in water.

"What are you doing?" she asked, staring at him.

He turned toward her and raised his eyebrows. "I'm washing dishes." He looked down his nose and added, "One does not put fine china and crystal through the dishwasher."

"I taught him that," Jane said proudly, drying the wet plate he passed to her.

Hilary had to grin. Her partner liked him. Jane didn't like everybody. "You'll lose your standing in the Male Chauvinists Club if the membership committee sees you like this."

He laughed. "I'm nice. Occasionally."

"Hell just froze over," she said, leaning her elbow

on the table and propping her head against her hand.

He grinned at her. "By the way, how's your grandfather?"

"Back in his shell." She shook her head. He was worse now than he'd been before the boat trip, and she didn't know why. "How's your grandmother?"

"Too brittle underneath."

Hilary groaned. It looked as if another "date" was needed. Just what she needed right now. Her muscles ached and her shoulders were stiff, all from tension, stress, and the double shock and mortification of Margo's tirade and Devlin's witnessing of it. Cold anger and a desire to show the woman some manners had kept her from losing her temper in front of everyone. It galled her, though, to know the woman had done it just to get out of paying a bill. Even though everything had turned out fine in the end, she wished she'd never taken the job. But Margo, with her list of social activities for the younger set, meant a new door of opportunity for clients.

She knew she should be clearing up, but she didn't move. Instead she watched Devlin at the sink. She was embarrassed and grateful for what he was doing. His offer to help had been so unexpected . . . and so needed. *Nice* wasn't a word she normally associated with him.

Seeing him now, surrounded by dishes, washing industriously, was a picture she'd never forget. Her heart filled and flipped over. She was more than grateful.

She was in love.

Hilary turned away, panic sweeping through her. She couldn't be, she thought frantically. Not Devlin Kitteridge. Of all people, not him. He was completely wrong for her. His lifestyle, his goals, his basic outlook on life were the exact opposite of hers. This wasn't love. All she felt was a flash of gratitude and affection for him.

She turned back and eyed him critically. The blinding-white shirt and tailored trousers he was wearing were a radical change from the jeans and T-shirt. But they didn't hide the width of his shoulders or the lean line of his body. Desire, slow and soft and strong, curled through her.

So much for critical, she thought. She had only to look at him anymore and her body would respond. *Affection* was too mild a term for what she was feeling. She'd never felt this way about her ex-live-in lover. It was why she had let him go.

It was the woman's curse, she thought, her heart sinking with certain knowledge. Nice, safe, compatible men were everywhere, right under women's noses, but they went for the wrong man every time. She wondered why. Was it because they were dangerous? Because they couldn't be trusted not to hurt one? Because they were a challenge? Because the combination of all of that made them exciting and worth the fight if the woman won?

All of the matchmaking nonsense they were doing had somehow pulled her in, she admitted. And naturally it wasn't that he'd swept her off her feet and into the bedroom that finally pushed her over the edge. No, she was a sucker for a man washing dishes.

"Hilary?"

She opened her eyes. Devlin was standing over her, so close that she could easily reach out and trace his features with her fingers, then urge his head lower until his lips touched hers.

"Thank you," she whispered.

"You're welcome." His tone was low and intimate.

Pain knifed through her, along with the need. It hurt to know how she felt . . . and how he didn't. He might want her at times, but he didn't like her. That he had made very clear.

"I need to pack up," she said, standing as she tried to force out the feelings within her and regain some composure.

It was a bad move. They were on kissing level now, only inches separating them.

His gaze never left her face, those damnable intense blue-green eyes probing beyond the surface. She'd never felt more vulnerable with him.

"I need to pack up," she repeated, her voice sounding hoarse to her ears.

"I'll help you," he said, not moving.

"You've helped enough already." Her feet were rooted to the floor. Panic flooded her again. She was aware of Jane and Jeremy in the room, but that didn't help her regain her control. She was positive Devlin was about to kiss her. She'd probably rip his clothes off him if he did.

Rescue came in the form of Lettice and Margo. The spell broke instantly as those two women entered the kitchen, and Hilary was able to turn and face them. Out of the corner of her eye she noticed Jane and Jeremy smirking at her. She'd never hear the end of it.

"Ah, there you are, Devlin," Lettice said, as if seeing her grandson in the kitchen with his sleeves rolled up were an everyday occurrence. "Hilary, dinner was superb, as always. Margo quite agrees. Don't you, dear?"

Margo's attempt at a smile was more like a

grimace of pain. "Yes. Well. Everyone was so pleased—"

"And still raving about the lamb," Lettice put in.

"And raving about the lamb," Margo repeated between clenched teeth. "I suppose the party wasn't completely ruined . . . so I suppose I will take care of the bill, after all."

Hilary refused to look at Lettice. She had no idea what the woman had done to bring about this change in her client, and she wasn't about to ask. Jeremy appeared like an unobtrusive magician, bill in hand. Margo, after a moment's hesitation, took it.

"You'll find it greatly reduced from what you were expecting to pay for the . . . before," Hilary said, avoiding mention of the sore point between them.

"Oh." Margo looked startled as she glanced at the bill. She nodded, then turned and walked out of the room.

"She'll pay it," Lettice said with satisfaction. "I let her know you had my complete patronage. I also let her know I thought she'd made an ass of herself, and I'd make sure everyone from Ritten-house Square to Gwynedd Valley knew it too."

Hilary felt almost sorry for Margo. For a person swiftly rising on the social fast track, having some-one of Lettice's stature against her was a huge black mark.

"You lost your sponsor," Devlin said to Lettice, then grinned. "I'm proud of you, Grandmother."

"High praise," Lettice said dryly.

"What sponsor?" Hilary asked.

"Never mind," Lettice said.

"She's been working on Richard, the husband,

to sponsor a charity ball for Villanova Hospital," Devlin said. "What the hell. I'll sponsor it."

His grandmother arched her eyebrows. "Well, well."

"No," Hilary said, everything in her protesting the idea. She'd be beholden to him beyond measure. "You can't. It's too much—"

"I've got a trust fund I never use," he said, looking puzzled. "At least I think I still do."

"You do," Lettice said.

"Right." His gaze returned to Hilary. "So, what's the problem?"

Everything, she thought. He'd have a stranglehold on her she'd never be able to break. The room wavered. Her legs turned to jelly, and she sat back down in the chair.

Devlin being "nice" was a revelation, one she wished she'd never seen.

Eight

"What!"

"I said I think your seeing Hilary is a mistake," Lettice repeated.

She watched her grandson's expression go from astonishment to anger as he nearly ran the car off the road.

"I thought you liked Hilary," he said, after straightening the car. He glanced over at her. "You certainly thought it was a good idea for me to find someone."

"I still do," she said. Now here came the tricky part, she thought. Things were poised on the brink—she could feel it. If she pushed wrong the least little bit, Dev would beat a hasty retreat. But she had to do something. Nature was entirely too slow to suit her. Carefully she added, "Unfortunately I've come to believe Hilary isn't . . . suitable for you."

"You mean she isn't suitable for *you*," Dev snapped. The car shot forward as his foot clamped down on the gas pedal.

"Slow down. My days may be numbered, but they're not up yet. And no, I do not mean that Hilary isn't suitable for me. She isn't suitable for you." She paused, staring at him. He stared back, his gaze intense, almost piercing. He wasn't bad at it, she thought. "Watch the road, or I will turn Eternity into a nightmare for you if you get us killed."

"Don't tempt me." But he did turn his attention back to the road. "You thought Hilary was a great idea until we went to that damn party tonight. What's the matter? Did you realize tonight that she doesn't 'fit in'?"

It was hard for Lettice to keep her lips clamped shut, but she did. It was better to let him "prove" her wrong.

"I knew it," he exclaimed. "Dammit, I knew that as soon as I spent more than five minutes with you, you would think you could run my life like you do the others. I'll see whoever I damn well please, Grandmother. This whole tradition of who's suitable and who isn't is ridiculous. I'm thirty-four years old, not some kid you can dictate to anymore. And you're a snob. The worst kind. Hilary's a damn sight better than some over-the-hill powder-puff deb you have in mind."

"She's not right for you," Lettice said stubbornly.

"And you're full of . . ." He stopped himself before using the barnyard curse. "Butt the hell out, Grandmother."

Lettice bristled. "You watch your language, Devlin."

He snorted, and the car sped up her driveway at breakneck speed. Lettice expelled her breath when Devlin braked to a screeching halt in front of her door. She had begun to wonder whether telling him in the car had been a good idea.

"You know I want only what's best for you," she said, deliberately uttering the parental words designed to set off a tantrum of rebellion in children the world over.

"Butt out," Devlin repeated between clenched teeth.

Lettice wisely vacated the car. It tore off in a squeal of tires, and she guessed her grandson wasn't staying the night after all. Bless Mr. Freud and his invention, she thought, smiling. Reverse psychology was a marvelous tool.

Now, if only it worked.

The pounding threatened to break down her front door.

Hilary scurried to it, tightening the belt of her flowered silk robe. In spite of the insistent banging, she peeked through the peephole first, then flung open the door.

"A simple knock would have sufficed," she told Dev.

"Not for this!" he snapped, stalking into the house.

Hilary had known she'd have to talk with him again eventually, but not, she would have hoped, as he was now. She'd never seen him so furious. Two hours ago at the dinner party he could have won the congeniality prize at the Miss America pageant. Now they'd be checking him for weapons at the door.

He spun around to face her. "I want you to find out every little grand ball, fancy party, and other hot spots my grandmother will be at."

"Why don't you ask her?" Hilary asked, eyeing him warily.

"Because I'm not talking to her!" he roared.

"I see," she said calmly.

"No, you don't." He ran his fingers through his hair and looked around, reminding her of a bull ready to charge. "Look, I'd like to take you to some of these things, so that my grandmother can see you. For the show."

She sensed there was more than the show involved here—especially at nearly one in the morning. "Devlin, I'm exhausted. Couldn't this wait until a more decent hour?"

He paused, then glanced at his watch. "I guess I forgot."

Hilary smiled ruefully and shook her head. There were times when she wondered if he ever thought with his brain, and this was one of them. A soft flutter of emotion welled up inside her. She forced it down. Devlin could shred a woman's feelings and not blink in the process. Still, since he was here, there was something she needed to do.

She drew in a deep breath, shut the door against the simmering night heat, and said, "Thank you for helping tonight. And for offering to take the place of the sponsor your grandmother wanted. But it's too much, Devlin. I—"

"No. It's a good cause." He waved his hand in dismissal. "Although it would serve her right if she lost me through her pigheadedness."

"That's what I wanted to talk with you about," Hilary tried again. "Jane and Jeremy and I have decided to be the ball's sponsors—"

"Don't be ridiculous," he said. "You don't have that kind of money."

"If we pool all our money, we should."

"No." He looked everywhere but at her. "I feel I have to—to make amends. I've said a lot of things to you that I shouldn't have."

"Are you sick?" she asked.

"No. Why would you think that?"

"Because you're not the bad old Devlin I've gotten used to."

His jaw hardened. "I was wrong. I'm apologizing. Just take it."

"Okay," she said shortly.

He relaxed and grinned at her. "Okay."

The silence began in amusement, but changed to something more intimate. He took a few steps forward, until only bare inches separated them. Hilary felt rooted to the floor, unable to look anywhere but at him. His mouth was a fascinating study . . . the slight thrust of his lower lip . . . the surprisingly soft words that fell from it. . . . She had to be mistaken in what she was feeling for him. It was just affectionate lust.

"I think we should go away together," he said.

Everything inside her suddenly became unglued. "What!"

He nodded. "I do. If we go away together, the grandparents are sure to follow."

"They're not lambs!" Hilary exclaimed, backing away from him.

Devlin grinned. "True. Still, yours will come to stop us, and mine will . . . Well, she hates to miss anything. Besides, it's the next logical step in our relationship."

"I thought you weren't talking to your grandmother," she said, her brain scrambling around in confusion.

The part of her that was hopeful wanted desperately to say yes. But her logical part knew better. She had the awful foreboding that she wasn't mistaken in her feelings after all. Suddenly the entire evening was too much. She leaned against the nearest wall, defeated.

"Think about it," he said, stepping closer. Alarm bells went off in Hilary as he added, "And while you're thinking, is there any chance of a cup of coffee? I have a long drive back to the shore."

"Of course," she murmured, then reached out and opened the front door. Much as she wanted to be, she wasn't a complete fool. Not yet. "The nearest diner is a quarter mile down the road."

He gazed at her with an injured expression. "Hilary, what would Miss Manners say about your kicking a guy out without even a cup of coffee?"

"That I was smarter than the average hostess."

"And after I striped plates and washed dishes for you."

"That's the breaks."

"I wasn't even supposed to go home tonight, but I can't stay at Grandmother's. . . ."

Her eyes widened at even the thought of what he was suggesting. "The nearest motel is two streets after the diner. Devlin!"

He shrugged and walked out the door, saying, "A man can dream, can't he?"

So could a woman, Hilary thought as she shut the door behind him. In her case she was worried she'd wake up to a nightmare.

Dev stared at the blank motel ceiling and cursed. He could have tried to kiss his way into her bed, he thought. There was a time when he would have done that without a qualm. But she'd seemed so tired and vulnerable, he'd had a pang of conscience. His conscience now satisfied, he couldn't believe he'd walked away from her.

Along with the frustration came the prospect of him and Hilary going away together. The thought had hit like lightning, and he had immediately acted upon it. Unfortunately he saw it was going to take some talking to get Hilary to come around. But he'd get what he wanted, and what he wanted was to be alone with her. There would be no show either. The grandparents would never find them. He'd ensure that.

Anger rose in him again as he thought of what his grandmother had said about Hilary that night. She'd been making judgments on people all of her life, but she was wrong on this one. How could she say Hilary was unsuitable for anyone? Couldn't she see that Hilary was more real than any of those phonies at the party? That she was making something of herself, and working hard for it? Couldn't his grandmother see the exciting combination of elegance and sensuality in Hilary?

Probably not, Dev admitted with a chuckle. The combination excited the hell out of him, though. In the beginning he would have sworn Hilary was the perfect match for his twin brother, Miles. Now he knew she stirred *him* physically and emotionally. She was suited to *him*. He snorted in disgust at what his grandmother had said.

That dinner party had been riddled with the class distinctions he'd long ago recognized as worthless. But his grandmother's complete reversal on Hilary puzzled him. He couldn't understand it. In these past few weeks, he'd come to like her a great deal, and he was disappointed that she'd been influenced by the party's atmosphere. Yet she'd come to Hilary's defense over the dinner. Why would she do that if she thought Hilary was unsuitable?

He'd considered telling Hilary what his grandmother had said, so that he could then tell her he disagreed. But he knew she would be hurt by the words. He couldn't do that to her. He never wanted to hurt Hilary again.

His grandmother needed to learn a lesson about people, Dev decided. In fact she needed to learn several lessons. It would serve her right if she got broadsided the way she'd broadsided him tonight. A wild notion entered his mind, and he smiled. Maybe there was something he could do to his grandmother after all.

"What!"

Dev nodded sadly as Marsh Rayburn stared at him with shock and indignation. He'd begun his grandmother's lesson bright and early this morning after.

"Yes, sir," Dev said. "I just wanted you to know that I completely disagree with my grandmother. Hilary is a fine woman, a wonderful woman, and if there's anyone who's unsuitable, it's me—"

"That old woman has gone too far!" Marsh roared, oblivious to Dev's words.

Dev nodded again, taking secret delight in hearing grand-dame Lettice Kitteridge called an old woman. Of course his grandmother would cut the heart out of anyone if *she* heard it. Yes, sir, Marsh was shaping up to be a fine cannon, and his grandmother was in the sights. He went on. "I couldn't believe it—"

"Let me tell you something, young man," Marsh

bellowed, clearly not listening. "I was engaged to your grandmother once. . . ."

"I know," Dev murmured.

". . . And she, treacherous snake that she is, didn't stand by me when my family lost all its money. Suddenly I was unsuitable. She couldn't break our engagement fast enough, and she couldn't get herself engaged to your grandfather fast enough. That's your grandmother, under her smooth, sophisticated surface. Love never counted a damn with her. Not if money wasn't attached to it."

Dev frowned. Despite his own anger with his grandmother, Marsh's assessment bothered him. Somehow it didn't quite sound like her. She'd always struck him as more the double-standard type—what she did and what others did were two different things. With her brand of willfulness, he couldn't imagine her giving up a man if she were in love with him. Maybe she hadn't loved Marshall in the past and that was why she'd broken off the engagement. Maybe the man had never wanted to accept that reason.

"I have had enough of her nonsense," Marsh said, pushing himself to his feet. He stomped out of his living room into the front hall. Dev followed, watching as Marsh grabbed keys off a side table. "I'm going to put a stop to all of this now. All that sweetness and light on the fishing trip and coming home. I knew it. I knew she couldn't be trusted. That's why I stayed away from her ever since. . . ."

"Ah, sir," Dev began, realizing the man was rambling.

Marsh kept on. "She'll regret she ever opened her mouth against my family. I'll make sure she learns a lesson she'll never forget."

Dev wondered if he'd stirred the man up a little too much. "Marshall . . ."

The older man turned, then blinked as if he'd completely forgotten Dev's presence. "Thanks for coming by, boy. I'm glad to see you're above your family's usual standards and you're standing by Hilary."

The words both pleased and annoyed Dev. "Well, my grandmother might just be a little confused. After all, at her age—"

"She ought to know better," Marsh finished, and strode out of his house.

"Who are you to say my granddaughter isn't suitable! She's a damn sight more suitable than your family deserves!"

Lettice gaped at Marshall, absolutely speechless. Less than two minutes ago he had roared up her driveway and roared into her home. She had expected her grandson to throw himself onto Hilary in a fit of rebellion. Instead he'd thrown Marsh at her. She had to give Devlin credit for one-upping her. And she had been wondering how to blast Marsh out of his hiding place since the fishing trip. This wasn't what she'd had in mind, however.

"Someone should have paddled you years ago, woman!" Marsh shouted, looming over her as she stood in the center of her sitting room.

"I never would have thought you were so kinky, Marshall," she said as she regained a shred of composure.

His eyes bulged and his face turned bright red. Obviously he was attempting to hold on to his temper. Lettice raised her chin in defiance. If she was going down for the count, it would be fighting all the way.

"You should be so lucky," he snapped. "How dare you say such a thing about my granddaughter."

Lettice tried a calm tone. "I like Hilary very much. I admire her greatly. But, Marsh, you've said yourself that Devlin and she aren't suitable—the last time you came blasting in here, remember?"

"I said your grandson wasn't suitable for my granddaughter. There is a *big* difference, and one that has nothing to do with your snobbish attitude."

"If one isn't suitable, then clearly the other isn't suitable," she argued logically. "Although your attitude is just as snobbish in its way. Still, you're right. They are not suitable for each other. I do not understand why you're fussing, now that I finally agree with you."

He shook his head in frustration. "Because you aren't agreeing with me. I told you once to leave my granddaughter alone, and I'm telling you now for the last time."

"But I *have* left Hilary alone." She gave him an arch look. "You're the one who's butted in. Look at you now, butting and fussing. Are you sure you're not protesting too much?"

Marshall stiffened. Lettice could see him struggle for words and braced herself. He looked like a volcano about to blow.

"Not! No! Ridic—!" He pointed a finger at her. "You!"

Then he turned and stormed out of the house.

Lettice let out her breath and sank gratefully into the nearest chair. She had never seen Marsh quite so mad before—and that was saying something. Devlin never should have repeated her words to him. She'd certainly never expected him to. That silly child, she thought, then corrected herself. *This silly old woman.* She never should have said it to Devlin in the first place. If Devlin had told Marshall, would he also tell Hilary? She hadn't considered that. The last thing she wanted was to hurt Hilary. She'd only thought to motivate her grandson. If she disapproved, then he would automatically approve. Maybe she was just a meddling old fool after all.

Mamie, her housekeeper, poked her head around the dining room archway. "You okay?"

Lettice nodded. "No bones broken."

"Lucky you."

Lettice gave Mamie her regal look. "I could cut your Christmas bonus."

Mamie sniffed. "You've been threatening that for thirty years."

"There's always a first time." Lettice smiled wryly. "By the way, I don't believe Dr. Rayburn will be having lunch with me."

"I had that feeling," Mamie murmured.

"I'm back," Devlin said.

"So I see," Hilary said.

"You did say we could talk in the morning," he reminded her.

"I did say that, didn't I."

"It's morning."

"Late morning."

"Still morning."

Two minutes more, Hilary thought in resignation, and she would have been gone. That is, if she hadn't overslept, she would have been gone. If she hadn't had a restless night, she wouldn't have overslept, and she would have been gone. If she hadn't thought she'd fallen in love, she wouldn't have had a restless night, and she wouldn't have overslept, and she would have been gone. . . .

Hilary got off the mental merry-go-round. She'd ridden one merry-go-round all night over what she was feeling for him, and she wasn't about to start another. Still, she opened the door wider and gestured for him to enter. Whatever she was feeling, she had come to a decision this morning. A decision she intended to keep.

Devlin walked inside. Hilary shut the door and instantly felt trapped. She had to force herself to turn around and face him.

He was wearing jeans and a soft chambray shirt, whose blue color intensified the startling contrast of his blue-green eyes and tanned skin. Rather than suppress, the clothes contributed to the sensuality he always exuded. She felt light-headed and more confused than ever. She walked past him and into her living room.

"I've thought about where we should go," he began, following her. "Somewhere that the grandparents would enjoy, feel comfortable in. So I eliminated Hedonism One and Two. However, a cruise would be ideal. You said you didn't get seasick on a cruise—"

"Devlin," she interrupted. "We need to talk about something else. Please, sit down."

Eyeing her warily, he sat on her sofa. To her surprise, he didn't slouch like the first time. She sat in a chair opposite him.

"I'm not going away with you," she said, folding her hands on her lap. "I'm not doing any more of this matchmaking. It's over."

"But why?" he asked.

He looked shocked, and that surprised her too. She had her answer ready, though. "Because we're not making progress with them. We're kidding ourselves that they'll ever get together. They're both too set in their ways. It's over, Devlin. We made a valiant try, but it's over."

"One lousy fishing trip is not a valiant try!" he argued.

"It's hopeless. Let's just admit it and be done."

"Has my grandmother talked to you this morning?" he asked.

"No," she said, puzzled. "Not since we left the dinner party. Why?"

"No reason." He stood up and began to pace the room. "Look, Hilary, I think our grandparents are worth all the effort we can put into them." He stopped in front of her chair and gazed down at her. "I think if we get them into a setting where they can't retreat to their respective corners as usual . . . where they're forced into each other's company over a period of time . . . they'll have to deal with each other. They've been lonely for a lot of years, too many years. Your grandfather's sinking into a deep depression: You said so yourself. Think of this as one all-out, last-ditch effort."

He looked so earnest, so pleading, that her heart flipped over. She forced herself to be strong. "Devlin, really. Nothing's worked so far—"

"Exactly!" he broke in. "Hilary, I've been . . . selfish about a lot of things. For a lot of years. I'd like to make it up . . . to a lot of people. My grandmother's one of them."

"I understand how you feel," she said slowly, trying to find the proper words. His own words nearly broke her willpower. "There are things I would like to make up to my grandfather. But there are things we can't make up. This is one of them."

"When the hell did you turn into me?" he asked, his hands clenching. "Dammit, you're not giving things a chance—"

Hilary couldn't stand it. She jumped up and started to walk out of the room. "I can't! I just can't!"

Devlin was after her, grabbing her arm and spinning her around before she reached the doorway. "Why can't you? I don't understand. . . ."

His voice trailed away as he stared into her eyes. Emotions, uncontrollable and irrepressible, ran through her. His body was so close to hers, the air between them felt squeezed.

"What's the problem, Hilary?" he asked, awareness glowing in his eyes. "This?"

His mouth covered hers.

Nine

Her mouth was soft, incredibly soft, even though he'd taken her by surprise. A man could easily lose himself in her and not resurface for days, Dev thought, pulling her closer. It was always like this with her.

As he'd looked into her eyes, he'd known what the problem was. It was her. She wanted him, and she was afraid of what he stirred in her. Even now her hands were clutching his upper arms, ready to push him away. But she didn't. She pressed her body more tightly to his.

He wanted her with an intensity that shocked him. He wanted everything with her.

She pulled back when he would have deepened the kiss, turning her face away and unintention-ally exposing the creamy flesh of her neck. He couldn't resist and planted tiny, almost biting kisses just under her ear, then soothed them away with his tongue.

She gasped, her nails digging into his muscles. The pleasure-pain they created was potent.

"Devlin, please."

"What do you want me to please?" he murmured against her warm skin. Why had he ever thought her cold?

"I don't know," she whispered back. Her hands crept up around his shoulders. "I shouldn't. I can't."

"Hilary, this isn't for show," he said, lifting his head and looking straight into her eyes. "The hell with the show. This is for us."

The moment the words left his mouth, he knew they sounded like a line, one of many he'd used without compunction on women in the past. He meant them this time, though, and he had the sinking feeling they would cause the rejection he was desperate to avoid.

A shudder ran through her, then her lips were on his again. Their tongues instantly mated, swirling together in a frenzy of need. His head spun with the sensations she created, and his blood pulsed thickly through his veins. He ran his hands down her spine, wanting to protect her and yet crush her to him at the same time. The way Hilary responded, beyond anything he had a right to expect, was a constant amazement for him. With each new thing he discovered about her, he was bound to her even more. She generated a lot of emotional bonds without even trying, and much as he had fought them, he hadn't been able to stop them. A deep satisfaction ran through him at the notion.

Every coherent thought flew out of his head as a little moan escaped her. He reached up and knotted his hands in her hair, pulling her head back and deepening the kiss even more. Minutes seemed to stretch into eternity as the sweet taste of her became his only focus. But then the need to touch skin, flesh to flesh, grew desperately.

"The bedroom," he gasped, burying his face in her hair. He tried to regain enough control to make their lovemaking proper, to take care of her. This was Hilary, and he wanted it perfect.

"No . . . here . . . now," she murmured.

"What?" He hadn't heard right, he thought dimly.

"Please, Devlin." Her mouth was on his again, like a white-hot fire.

"But . . ."

Without another word she pulled him down to the living room floor.

Protests and questions were on his lips, but he resisted the urge to say them. He didn't know what had happened to the Ms. Prim Hilary he knew, but he didn't want the magic to stop.

Clothes disappeared in a fumble of fingers. He touched her everywhere, kissed her everywhere, grateful for the gift she was giving him. Her skin was soft, softer than he'd ever imagined. Her breasts fit his hand as if made for him, the nipples tight with her need. He traced them with his tongue, teased them with his lips, pulled first one, then the other into his mouth, tasting the honeyed flesh. He traced the curves of her body, and the satiny feel of her skin drove his control to the breaking point.

Hilary clawed at him, giving herself up to the sensations Devlin created within her. A primitive wildness rampaged through her, and she couldn't stop, even if she wanted to. And she didn't. Not now, not ever. All her resistance had evaporated the moment he looked at her and knew what she was trying to deny. She had known, too, that he'd meant it when he said this was just for them. Those words had broken the final barrier for her. Their desire had grown despite the way they fought each other, and neither of them could resist any longer. She had never taken any true risks in her life. She had never wanted to—until now. It might be, just might be, that Devlin felt the same way she did. She couldn't risk not having that. She couldn't wait any longer.

His hands sparked a blinding heat as his mouth lifted her to the brink of sensual insanity. His skin was like smooth, hard steel beneath her hands. She delighted in the feel of the dark, silky hair that covered his chest, and she traced the line of it down beyond his waist. She tested her hands against the firm muscles of his thighs, the rougher hair of his legs almost tickling the sensitive flesh of her palms.

His fingers caressed her thighs, then found the inner softness of her, stroking her until she was groaning and writhing with her need of him. It was instinctive for her to give him the same kind of pleasure, to feel the same kind of need in him. The unique scent of him filled her nostrils, imprinted itself forever on her brain. She could taste his heat on her lips. Just when she thought she would explode from denial, he pulled her under him and plunged inside her.

She gasped at the way every inch of them fit perfectly together . . . at the rightness of it. Nothing had ever felt so right before. He buried his face in her neck. His lips were feverish on her skin, his breath hot and rasping. They moved together instantly, triggered by the same internal signals. They ebbed and flowed as one, the love swirling in and out as they surrendered to the eternal intimacy that bound man and woman to each other. Hilary clung to Devlin, and he clung to her, as emotions and need clashed together in a final crescendo, bringing them to the quiet peace of oblivion.

Long minutes later Hilary became aware of Devlin's body lying heavily on hers and the total contentment his weight brought. Nothing but contentment, she thought with a lazy smile.

"You shock the hell out of me sometimes," he said, his voice muffled as he kissed her neck. "Every time."

"Thank you," she said primly, then laughed.

He laughed with her, and their laughter grew. They held each other tightly, sharing the release their amusement brought. Eventually it subsided, and they lay quietly together, the intimacy complete. Whatever regrets or doubts Hilary might have felt had dissipated. She wasn't going to think of them any longer, she decided, knowing she was long past the danger mark. She would just take what was offered. For a man like Devlin, sometimes that was all there was.

"I suppose I ought to be a gentleman," he finally said, and rolled onto his back, pulling her on top of him.

She crossed her arms over his chest, her fingers absently toying with the dark hairs at the base of his throat.

"Do I have to be a lady now?"

"Hell, no." He ran his hands down her back, then sank his fingers into her derriere and pressed her hips to his. "You can always be very bad with me."

"Good." She stretched up and kissed him lightly on the lips, the motion leaving him gasping for breath. Then she kissed the side of his mouth, his jaw. She traced his jawline with her tongue, feeling the slight scratch of a whisker or two that he'd missed shaving that morning.

Devlin growled and urgently brought her mouth to his.

"By the way, did you have anything to do today?" Dev asked. It was nearly two o'clock and they were in her kitchen, the need for food having finally overcome the need for love. She was dressed in his shirt and her underwear. Wearing only his jeans, he leaned against a counter, rubbed his naked chest, and decided she looked sensational.

"No. Did you have anything to do?" Hilary asked, opening the refrigerator door. She bent over to get something from the back of the fridge.

"Don't do that!" he exclaimed, as desire, sudden and fierce, pounded through him at her innocent stance. Their lovemaking had clearly opened a sensual Pandora's box, one he hoped would never close.

She turned around. "What? You don't want leftover lamb?"

"No." He grinned. There was no sense telling her what she did to him. She might not do it anymore. "I'm hungry enough to eat the lion too."

She laughed. "I do have a hunter's recipe—"

"Never mind," he said quickly. He wouldn't put it past her to whip up a predator's stew. "Haven't you ever heard of junk food?"

"My grandfather asks me that." She walked over to the stove and he watched her do ordinary things with that natural elegance only she had.

"You are going away with me," he announced, suddenly remembering his real reason for coming to see her that morning. Then he added cautiously, "Aren't you?"

She smiled at him. "I suppose I have to. You'll drag me away in a caveman tactic if I don't."

He chuckled. "Probably."

She turned back to the food. "Why is your boat called the *Madeline Jo*?"

His stomach knotted in sudden tension. What would she think of him after he told her what had happened so long ago? Her opinion of him mattered more than he wanted to admit. He didn't care if everyone else in the world thought he was a bastard, so long as Hilary didn't. There was a time when he would have thought it impossible to care, and now it seemed impossible not to.

He walked up behind her and touched her hair, stroking it away from her face. Leaning forward, he rested his chin on her shoulder. "I named it the *Madeline Jo* to remind myself that I once was very stupid and it cost someone his life, and to remind myself never to be so stupid again."

"Tell me." The words were simple, quiet.

And so he told her everything about that summer, more than he'd thought of in years. She listened without interruption, then turned around in his arms when he was finally finished. She put her hands on his shoulders.

"Get with it, Devlin," she said, though not without some sympathy. "It was an accident, pure and simple. And it's past time to let the guilt go and stop punishing yourself and everyone else for it."

He gaped at her. "You think that's what I've been doing? Have you ever been responsible for someone's death?"

"No." She smiled a gentle smile. "But that doesn't mean I can't have some objectivity about it.

You can't change the past or bring anyone back. And you've atoned long enough. You've more than earned the right to move on with your life."

"But I like my life," he said. "I don't want to go back."

"Then don't. Just be happy with yourself."

Her words disturbed him, shuddering through the foundation of his world. He hadn't wanted her to lose the feelings she had toward him, but he hadn't expected her to take him to task for doing the right thing for *too* long.

She kissed him. "You never did answer my question."

"What question?" he asked absently. Her breasts were pressing into his chest and her hands were caressing his shoulders, distracting him from memories of the past.

"Did you have anything to do today?"

"Just a charter or two . . ." Her mouth was on his collarbone, evoking sensations that blocked coherent thought. "How long's this stuff gonna take to cook?"

She reached around behind her. He heard the click of the oven being turned off. "A long time."

"I won't hurt you," he said, feeling the need to make that promise. Hilary had let her barriers down with a clang, and he knew the trust she'd given him that day. He would never abuse it. He couldn't.

She nestled closer to him in answer. He held her tightly, just held her, and then the primitive urges started all over again, even stronger this time. When he would have led her upstairs to the bedroom, she stopped him.

"I saw this movie once," she murmured. "*Bull Durham*. They made love on the kitchen table. . . ."

Dev immediately turned and swept the bowl of flowers from the kitchen table. "Just keep shocking the hell out of me," he said as he pulled her down onto it.

"I promise."

And she did.

"Finally," Devlin said as Hilary curled up against him under the covers of her bed, "in the bed, like all good couples should."

"So you're saying I'm a wanton," she said, pleased with the idea. She felt lethargic and content and incredibly sensual.

"Absolutely," he replied, sounding lethargic and content and incredibly sensual too.

It was after lunch, at last, and they were supposed to be taking a nap. She had a feeling they wouldn't get that far. At least, she hoped so.

She was glad that she now knew the real reason for his boat's name. It was none of the unrequited-love fears she'd had. She also understood much better why he tried to keep people at a distance—a great distance. Just as he had said he would never hurt her, she vowed never to hurt him. A little voice reminded her that while she didn't want to hurt him because she loved him, he didn't want to hurt her because he didn't.

As she mulled over that unpleasant bit of reality, Devlin began to chuckle.

"What's so funny?" she asked.

"I was just thinking of what your grandfather would say if he saw us like this."

She giggled. "I think he'd be speechless."

"I think he'd go, 'round the bend." He began to laugh. "And my grandmother. Did I tell you she's decided we're unsuitable after all? She told me that last night."

"Last night . . . ?" Hilary thought back to his visit of the night before, when he'd been furious with Lettice. It seemed like ages ago. "But she thought we were a good idea in the beginning, when she thought she was matchmaking us. Why would she change her mind?"

"Hell, who knows?" He shrugged. His amusement hadn't faded, though, since he chuckled again. "She was dead wrong, wasn't she?"

Somehow his words weren't reassuring. Instead they set off a vague warning bell inside Hilary. She frowned.

"Do you remember that first dinner?" he asked. "Did you want me as much as I wanted you when you were stabbing me with your spoon?"

She smiled. "I must have. I was so angry with you."

"And I was a complete gentleman." He grinned wolfishly. "More fool I."

"Serves you right."

"Maybe we shouldn't go on a deadly dull cruise. Hedonism One and Two are more and more appealing."

"What are Hedonism One and Two?"

He shook his head. "Hilary, Hilary, Hilary. It's an all-adult resort. Single adults."

"Ah. I see. Sybaritic pleasures across the board."

"Yep. It might be interesting to see what the grandparents would do in a place like that."

She laughed. "Probably a lot more than you think."

"That's a scary notion."

"I thought we had a notion to go to sleep."

He rolled her over onto her back, trapping her

hands with his above her head. "You've turned me into a satyr."

"As long as it's something cheerful."

He pressed his hips against hers. "I'm very cheerful. See?"

"I don't want to go," Devlin said, pulling her into his embrace.

It was early evening, and they were standing by her front door. He had a charter first thing in the morning, and they both knew he couldn't stay longer. He'd already missed that day's charter.

Hilary rested her cheek against his shoulder. "I know. I don't want you to go."

"Come with me," he said.

She closed her eyes against the temptation. "I can't. I have a dinner to do tomorrow night."

"Can't Jane and Jeremy handle it?"

"It's a big one. What about your first mate? Can he take the charter tomorrow?"

"No, he and his wife are going away to see their children. Damn!"

"Can you come up after your charter?" she asked hopefully.

"I have one the next morning too. Summer is my busiest time. What about Friday?"

"A dinner again." Her heart began to sink. Their basic lifestyles were at extremes again. The thought was upsetting. Worse, she was terrified that if she were out of sight, she'd be out of mind. What she shared with Devlin was too fragile to survive that. But she wasn't going to demand, or beg, or cling. She sensed those tactics would drive him away.

"Okay," he said, rubbing her arm in consolation,

"let's be yuppies and get out our damn appointment books. When's the next time you're free?"

"Saturday. And I'm free Sunday too."

"I'll make sure I'm free Sunday. And maybe Monday." He kissed her longingly. "We'll work this out. Now that I've found out how suitable we really are, I'm not about to let you go. And I don't want you to let me go."

The words sang through her. She wanted to ask him if he meant them, but resisted the urge. He'd said them and that was enough.

The second kiss held more longing and more hunger. It took a tremendous amount of willpower for her not to beg or cling . . . or go with him. She couldn't leave her clients in the lurch any more than he could leave his.

Two hours after he left, her phone rang. She snatched it up.

"I'll tell you what's unsuitable. It's this damn empty bed," Devlin said.

"So's this one." Hilary smiled, pleased that he'd called the moment he'd gotten in and pleased by his words. The doubt and worry, which had crept in after he'd left, faded.

But when she eventually hung up, her contentment and yearning began to wane. She was increasingly bothered by one word—*unsuitable*.

He'd used it again. She was a little hurt that Lettice had decided she and Devlin weren't a good pair. She had to admit they were an *odd* couple, so she could understand Lettice's concern. Her grandfather had been spouting it from the beginning, after all. Of course he was prejudiced.

She shrugged it away and concentrated on the change in Devlin. It had been remarkable, and that gave her hope. He'd let her past the walls he'd erected, something she never would have expected to happen. They were such opposites, too, but that didn't seem to matter anymore. Except for their jobs, she thought. Eventually, if their relationship progressed, they would have to work on that.

Why, she wondered, didn't Lettice approve of them any longer? What had changed the woman's mind last night? It shouldn't matter. What did matter was that Devlin's mind had changed. . . .

Hilary swallowed back a lump of uneasiness. Did one relate to the other? Now that "the family" disapproved, he didn't? She shouldn't care what had started him on this new course, she told herself firmly. She should only care that he had. She wouldn't question it any longer. She would just accept it.

She had to.

Ten

"The charter I missed was rescheduled for Sunday," Dev said to Hilary over the phone the next day. "Billy assumed that's what I'd want. Normally I do. But not this time. I would have told you about it before when I called, but I didn't see Billy's note until now. I'll try to change it if I can."

Even as he said the words, he knew it would be impossible. He was booked solid until Labor Day, except for the odd day off. His heart sank at her next words.

"No, don't" she said. "You've lost enough business as it is. Even if you can afford it financially, you can't afford it in terms of reliability. I'll come down Saturday afternoon . . . and stay. If you like."

"I more than like," he murmured, grateful to have gotten his secret wish. "I miss you."

He'd never meant those words more. He did miss her. At first he he'd resisted the conspiracy to get them together, and now that he was no longer resistant, everything seemed to be conspiring to keep them apart.

"I miss you too," she said, her voice low and incredibly sexy.

The quiet ones were a surprise, he thought happily. Why had he passed them by before? What had he been missing? Maybe not much, he conceded. Maybe it was just Hilary.

"You promise you'll come," he said, suddenly worried that the quiet ones might change their minds.

"Yes. I promise."

"Good." Still, he knew he wouldn't feel completely at ease until she was on his boat and in his arms. "I'm really sorry about this, Hilary. I'd like to strangle Billy, but he's in Michigan. We'll work this out. I promise."

"It's just a busy time for both of us."

"And the first time we've had to deal with this, I suppose." He was grateful she was being so understanding. "You'll drive down carefully. It's a long ride and tiring. You'll be by yourself—"

"You keep being this solicitous and you'll make me think I've got the wrong number." The amusement in her voice took any sting out of her words.

He laughed ruefully. "Okay, so you know my secret. I'm a mother hen at heart."

"And I'm the Frugal Gourmet."

"I hope not," he said, thinking of the thin, bearded man with the piping voice he'd watched at bleary-eyed times during long winter layovers. "He isn't as sexy as you are."

"Devlin, I'll be fine."

"Okay. We'll plan our getaway so that the grandparents can follow us in hot pursuit. Can you pick up brochures and stuff from a travel agent?"

"Yes."

"Good."

Just as he hadn't wanted to leave the previous day, he didn't want to break the connection with her. Unfortunately work reared its ugly head. He was beginning to hate work, he decided, as he hung up the phone.

But they would figure something out, he vowed. And that was a promise.

Hilary almost didn't make it.

From her perch on the hood of her car she watched the *Madeline Jo* approach the dock. Vast relief washed through her, along with instant anxiety. The long drive had caused a decrease in her courage and an increase in doubts, and she'd nearly turned back twice. When she'd arrived at Wildwood and seen that the boat was still out, she'd been ready to run once more. Now the nervousness and doubts were back. What if he didn't want her, after all?

She wouldn't know until she went down there and found out, she told herself. But maybe she didn't want to know. She took a deep breath and put the thought from her mind. She slid off the car and got her things from the trunk. The small overnight bag and the picnic basket felt like lead weights dragging on her arms, while her feet seemed barely able to manage a slow trudge. She would probably look like Magilla Gorilla by the time she reached the boat, she thought. She should have checked her hair. And her lipstick. And her summer dress for wrinkles. What if she got seasick again? It didn't matter that the boat would be tied up at the dock. The potential was there. Please, she prayed, not that humiliation.

When she finally reached the slip where the

Madeline Jo was berthed, Dev's charter group was climbing down the gangplank rungs. The closed ranks of machismo permeated the air surrounding the five men. She wished she'd waited until they'd left before she'd come down to the dock.

"Hey, Dev!" one of them called. "You've got a visitor."

The men hooted. "Yeah, a visitor," another said. "You better not go trolling with a weakie, buddy!"

This was not going well, Hilary thought with a silent moan of embarrassment.

"That's enough," Devlin said, his tone good-natured and his voice brooking no further comment. The men shuffled sheepishly, then nodded in apology as they walked past her.

Devlin grinned at Hilary. "Don't mind the slobs. They just want to bask in a last moment of being macho men before going home to become henpecked husbands."

She smiled. He looked happy to see her. Very happy. Relief shot through her. She could forgive the men their crude remarks this once.

Devlin stepped onto the dock and pulled her to him, his lips instantly on hers in a long kiss. Hilary's doubts dissolved as the warm fire inside her promised to burst into a white-hot heat. When he finally lifted his head, he said, "Damn, but you feel good."

"So do you." It didn't matter that her arms were hanging at her sides because of the packages she carried. All that mattered was that she was where she wanted to be.

"Come aboard." He took the heavy picnic basket from her and held it up. "Leftovers? Again? I can't wait."

She laughed. "Actually it's duck salad from the

Magnolia Café, foie gras from Assouline and Ting, rolls from the Lanci Bakery, carrot cake from the Carrot Cake Man, ribs from the Rib Crib, and soft pretzels from Fishers in the Reading Terminal."

"What? No veggies?"

"They're in the carrot cake."

Devlin sighed. "My kind of unsuitable woman."

I hope so, she thought, as he helped her onto the boat. She was staking her emotional sanity on it. She shook off the idea that she was staking too much on something that had too many odds against it, although she mentally winced at the word *unsuitable*. It was only a word, she told herself, and it meant nothing.

The deck was a mess from the aftermath of fishing and gutting. "I haven't had a chance to clean up yet," Devlin said. "I hope you can bear with it for a few more minutes."

She smiled. "Don't worry about it. I've seen the inside of a fish before."

"We'll get your stuff stowed, then I'll come out and clean it up."

Once inside the cabin, the wanting and need immediately broke to the surface. They were in each other's arms, their mouths coming together in a hungry kiss, while the gangway door was still swinging closed. His hands were all over her, almost desperate, as if attempting to assure himself she was real and there with him. Hilary forgot everything, as the suppressed longing surged through her like a raging river through opened floodgates.

"I thought you were going to clean up," she whispered, then gasped in pleasure as his hands cupped her breasts.

"Eventually," he murmured.

The afternoon was spent in love.

Later, much later, as they lay on his narrow bed, Dev stretched lazily and said, "I like your version of 'A loaf of bread, a jug of wine and thou.' But all you really needed to bring was thou."

She snuggled closer, her body naked and warm and languid next to his. He sighed in pleasure.

"If you don't get the bread and jugs away in the fridge, it might just be 'thou,'" she said, not moving.

"Thou is fine. And there's a take-out place on the pier. We're set for life."

At one time those words would have been scary, he thought, but now they had a nice ring to them.

"I suppose we ought to get up," she said.

He tightened his hold on her. "Nope."

"If we put those things away, then there won't be a single interruption afterward. . . ."

"And then we can be unsuitable again?"

"Absolutely."

He let her go. She got up and threw on his shirt. Dev didn't know whether to be disappointed or amused by her automatic need to cover herself. He admitted he would have been shocked if she hadn't. And Hilary was shocking enough when she wanted to be. Still, he was intensely pleased that she had picked his shirt to wear.

"Well?" she said. "Aren't you getting up? You've still got a deck to clean too."

"You've got my clothes," he pointed out. "If you take off my shirt—"

"Never mind," she said primly, and walked out of the room.

He sighed, then called out, "Did you get some brochures?"

"Yes, Master."

"Good. Bring them in when you come back."

"Your manners are atrocious, Devlin Kitteridge."

He chuckled. "Think of me as virgin territory you can mold."

She walked back around the corner of the door and leaned against the wall. "Speaking of molding, I saw this movie called *Ghost*. . . ."

"I'll buy a potter's wheel," he promised.

"You'd better buy a potter's steam roller if we're going to mold you." She turned and went back into the galley.

One up for her, Dev thought happily. "Are you trying to provoke me, woman?"

"Get out here and help me and I promise to provoke you beyond your wildest dreams."

He was up in a flash and striding into the galley.

Hilary looked up from rummaging through the basket on the counter. Her cheeks turned pink. "Devlin, you're naked."

"I just want to be ready for when you provoke me," he explained, taking a package out of the basket. "Where do you want this?"

"Fridge."

He squeezed past her in the narrow space. Only the thin cotton of his shirt separated his flesh from the softness of her derriere, and he loved it.

"You know," he drawled. "If you'd been wearing this when we were cramped in here on that fishing trip with the grandparents, we would have been halfway to Iceland before I got out of the galley. Nope, I'm wrong. It would have been all the way to Iceland."

"Not with my stomach," she said, leaning back against him.

"How is it?"

"Fine." She didn't move, however. Her body was still pressed tightly to his.

"Keep this up and we'll be testing a personal theory I'm formulating about exactly what one can cook in here."

"More than you think," she murmured, but finally let him pass. He sighed in disappointment as she added, "Put away the ribs, please."

"With pleasure."

She handed him several more things to load into the tiny refrigerator.

"Do you think you brought enough?" he asked, eyeing the stream of packages passing through his hands.

"Have you ever seen a movie called *Tom Jones*?" she asked innocently.

He stared at her in wonder. "The eating scene?"

"The eating scene."

"What other unsuitable movies are we going to do?" he asked.

"Wait and see."

It would be one eye-opening weekend, Dev decided.

He couldn't have asked for more.

"What do you think of the Micky Mouse cruise?" Hilary asked that evening, picking up one of the vacation brochures spread out on the bed.

"Too much fun," Dev said. He was sprawled naked on top of the covers, eating ribs. He stripped some meat off the bone with his teeth and in between chewing added, "We want the grandparents to get together, not zoom around on the Dumbo ride."

She laid the open brochure across the junction of his legs. "One down."

"Wanna bet?"

"You are disgusting," she pronounced, smiling fondly.

"I am a sybaritic pleasure in the making."

"You are a sybaritic mess." Whatever worries Hilary had started out with were gone in the afterglow of an idyllic afternoon and evening. She was almost able to ignore even the few bumps of *unsuitable*. Almost. She still couldn't quite shake the feeling that she'd become a point of rebellion for him.

Forget it, she told herself. For a point of rebellion, she'd never felt so thoroughly loved. They had the rest of the weekend together—with a time-out for his charter of course—and she wouldn't ruin it with even one doubt. Picking up another brochure, she said, "How about this Caribbean Hopper cruise?"

Dev glanced at it. "Too many port stops, therefore too many opportunities for one or both of them to get off and fly back to the States. We need something that keeps them away from transport until they don't care anymore."

She laid it on top of the first brochure. "Two down."

"You're going to give me a complex," he complained.

"In a pig's eye." She sifted through the pile, grumbling, "Do you know how many travel agents I had to go to in order to get all these damn brochures?"

"No. How many?"

"Two."

"That many?"

"How many did you go to?"

"Zip."

"Then shut up and let me complain."

A Cruise to Nowhere. They both spied the same brochure at the same time and grabbed for it. Hilary pried it out of his barbecue-sauced fingers. "Look at this mess you—*Look at this*!" she exclaimed.

He set aside the plate and leaned forward, looking over her shoulder. "I see it."

Together they read, "Two weeks to absolutely nowhere, while being pampered by our staff. Luxury beyond belief. Nobody does it better than the *Inca Lines*."

"They'll be bored to tears in two days," Devlin said with great satisfaction.

"Less."

"The next one's scheduled in two weeks. I'll talk to Billy when he gets back tomorrow about taking the charters. Let's try to book for that one, okay?"

She nodded. "I've got a couple of dinners and two luncheons. I'll talk to Jane and Jeremy, too, but I don't see a problem."

"Well, our work is done." He put his arms around her from behind, his hands stroking her thighs. As he kissed the curve of her neck, he murmured, "Time for play."

"You're getting barbecue sauce on me," she said, breathless with the sensations he was creating.

"I'll lick it off."

"I was hoping you'd say that."

And they sank into each other's arms, their bodies dancing to the night music of love.

"Wake up! Hilary, wake up!"

Bleary from a dead-to-the-world sleep, Hilary

opened her eyes. She winced and immediately shut them against blinding light overhead. She had a vague notion of Devlin, fully dressed, looming over her.

"Hilary, wake up! I forgot to set the alarm, and we overslept. The guys are here. You have to go."

"Guys? Go?" She squinted one eye in the direction of his voice. Her senses told her it wasn't even close to a normal morning hour yet.

"The charter group's here, and you can't stay. You get seasick, remember? Dammit, come on!"

She opened both eyes at his impatience. Every bone in her body felt like jelly. "What are you talking about? Why do I have to go? What time is it?"

He threw her underwear on her lap. "I'm talking about my Sunday charter. They're here, and you have to go because you can't go out with us. And it's a little after five-thirty."

She bolted upright. "In the morning!"

He grinned. "You're finally with it. I've packed up everything for you."

"Wait a minute. Are you telling me I have to leave immediately because of your charter?"

"Yes." He frowned in puzzlement. "You don't expect to stay, do you? You'd be uncomfortable, and they'd be ticked that I have a woman on board when they're not allowed to bring their own. Besides, you get seasick."

She stared at him in disbelief. "But I thought I was coming for the whole weekend. Why didn't you tell me about this?"

"I told you about the charter, although I didn't even think about your having to leave until the guys showed up this morning," he admitted. "I just assumed . . . I don't know what I assumed. That you thought of it when I didn't?"

"Well, I didn't."

"I'm sorry." He patted her arm. "But you can't stay on for the charter. We won't be too long."

"Only half the day," she said ruefully, then took a deep breath to orient herself. Her body was screaming for more sleep. She ignored it. "Okay. I just need some coffee—"

"No time," Devlin said, tossing the rest of her clothes at her. "The guys are waiting on deck. Hilary, please. They're a group of pain-in-the-butt executives with a time clock running. This is not a patient bunch. The only reason I take them on is because their checkbooks flow."

"Can I at least go to the bathroom?" she asked.

He smiled apologetically. "Do you really have to?"

"Devlin!"

"I'm sorry, I'm sorry."

She took another deep breath. "Okay. I'll be ready in five minutes."

He kissed her soundly on the mouth. "You are terrific. I'll go up and tell them."

He hurried out of the room. Hilary got up and staggered to the head, cursing under her breath the entire time. This was *not* the weekend she'd had in mind. She looked longingly at the shower, calculated the odds, then sighed in resignation. She had just pulled on her clothes and was about to brush her teeth and hair, when there was a pounding on the door.

"Ready? It's been five minutes," Devlin called through the varnished wood door.

"No, I'm not ready yet!"

"Okay, but hurry up."

She deliberately took her time brushing her

hair. She examined her teeth closely to see if they needed flossing. One did need to floss regularly. She finally decided she could forgo it this once, but she brushed thoroughly, ten times for each tooth.

"Hilary, please!" Devlin begged for the fifth time.

She took one last look in the mirror, smoothed back her hair, then opened the bathroom door. She smiled sweetly. "I'm ready."

"Great. You're being terrific about this. Let's go." He reached out and pulled her across the threshold. She nearly lost her balance, but he yanked her upright and hustled her down the hall, through the saloon, and up the gangway. Her head was spinning by the time they reached the last step.

She wasn't prepared for running the gauntlet of sport fishermen standing on the *Madeline Jo*'s deck. The predawn hour was a dead giveaway to what she and Devlin had been doing. Some of the men looked amused, some looked disgusted. Humiliation heated her cheeks, and she scurried past them, keeping her head down.

Devlin helped her onto the dock, then handed over her things. "I'm really sorry about this."

She nodded.

He kissed her on the cheek, then turned around to the men. "Are we ready to go, gentlemen?"

"We've been ready since Monday, Kitteridge," one snapped.

As Devlin leaped up to the fly bridge, Hilary remained on the dock gaping, shocked at the way he'd dismissed her. She knew he had to take care of his clients, but he didn't have to be this abrupt. Fury and hurt wound through her, but she'd be damned before she'd let it show.

She raised her chin and walked serenely away.

Eleven

He was in big trouble.

Dev drew in a deep breath, shifted the load of roses in his arm, and rang the doorbell to Hilary's town house. Nobody answered. He glanced over at her car in her parking slot, then leaned on the doorbell.

Finally the door opened. Hilary was wearing her flowered silk robe and her hair was mussed. Clearly he'd awakened her. She stared at him.

"I'm sorry," he said, holding out the roses. "I was a jerk . . . and a cad . . . and a rude pig . . . and can you ever forgive me?"

She looked at the roses.

"This is a really big apology for me," he pointed out.

"True." She took the roses.

Relieved, he said, "Can I come in and debase myself further? I drove all this way right after the guys left in order to do it."

"I suppose."

He stepped through the door and shut it behind him. "I thought you'd be there when I got back."

"I was supposed to stay at my car and wait for *you*?" She thrust the roses back at him.

"Ah . . . well . . ." he said helplessly, scrambling to find better words. He gave up. "Oh, hell, Hilary. It was a mess, and I'm sorry."

She took the roses back.

He pulled her into his arms and kissed her hair. "We'll learn."

"I don't know, Devlin," she whispered.

"Don't say that!" he admonished, tilting her head back and searching her eyes. "We both have businesses to run, and we're just having a little trouble coordinating ourselves. We can work all this out—if we want to. You *do* want to, don't you?"

"Yes," she said firmly. "But—"

"No *but*s." He kissed her mouth. "You've got to have some faith, Hilary. I do. This morning was bad, that's all. And that's the worst it will ever be. I promise."

She leaned against him. "Then I suppose I forgive you. We'll try."

"We *will*." He yawned. "Want company for a nap? I can nap until tomorrow night. Billy's taking tomorrow's charter."

"Sure we'll nap?" she asked.

"It's a fifty-fifty possibility," he said, all too aware of her body, lithe and distracting, against his.

Later he decided it was a good thing he didn't bet.

"Devlin and I are going away," Hilary said to her grandfather over the phone the next morning.

"You're what!"

Hilary held the receiver away from her ringing ear and made a face.

"And I thought he was beginning to like me," Devlin mouthed to her from across the breakfast table.

"He's coming around," she mouthed back, and brought the receiver to her ear again. "Now, Grandfather, don't spoil things for me. It's a wonderful two-week cruise to nowhere—"

"With *your* stomach?" His voice, at least, had lowered to a dull roar.

"I don't get seasick on the big cruises. You know that," she reminded him. She had been seasick once, she thought, and now nobody would let her forget it.

"I'm very disappointed in you, Hilary."

"And I am disappointed in you," she returned, bristling. "I'm an adult, capable of making my own decisions. Stop treating me like a child." She softened her voice. "Be happy for me, Grandfather. That's all I ask."

"Mmmph. Well, I suppose he's not *that* bad, although it's a shame he's related to that . . . that old—"

"Grandfather!" she admonished, while Dev made a thumbs-up in agreement. Men were all alike, she thought. "I wanted to give you the information so that you would know where I was in case you need to get hold of me."

His sigh of resignation came clearly over the line. "All right, let me get a pen."

When he was ready, she dictated the cruise itinerary to him.

"A cruise to nowhere," he said when she was through. "I have to admit it's an intriguing idea. I wonder how many people go on those things. . . ."

Hilary grinned. He had taken the bait. When she

hung up the telephone a few minutes later, she said to Devlin, "You're next."

"You had the easy part," he said, taking the phone from her.

"My ear will never be the same."

He dialed his grandmother's number. "Do you think he'll book?"

"I think he's calling the travel agent right now."

"Good. . . . Hello, Grandmother? It's me, Dev." He made a face. "Yes, the stranger. You just saw me last week. . . . Well, I . . . Never mind. Grandmother, Hilary and I are going away together on a two-week cruise to nowhere."

Hilary wished desperately that she could hear the other end of the conversation, but Lettice didn't bellow like her grandfather did. As she watched, Dev's expression hardened. Her heart froze.

"Thank you, Grandmother. I'll keep it in mind." His voice was as stern as his features. She could easily discern the anger he was suppressing. "I only wanted to let you know where I'd be after next week. . . ."

"What did she say?" Hilary asked after he'd hung up.

"The usual. Grandmothers do not change. Give them what they want and suddenly they don't want it." He seemed to shudder, as if shaking off something mentally, then grinned at her. "I guess we'd better book this cruise before we get left at the dock."

She forced herself to smile. "I guess we'd better."

As Devlin called the travel agent, she wondered what Lettice had said. Perhaps something yet again about how they weren't suitable for each other. She tried not to let it bother her, but she couldn't help it. What had she done that had so offended Lettice? Or was Devlin right? Could Lettice be one of those perverse people who never wanted something once they got it? Lettice could fit that mold, Hilary acknowledged. Was it possible that Dev wasn't rebelling, but that Lettice was?

Either way, Hilary thought, it only left *her* more confused than ever.

Devlin hung up the phone, then walked around the table and pulled her into his arms.

He nuzzled her hair and murmured, "All booked."

She forced her growing apprehension aside. Maybe she was the one with the hang-ups. And if she was, then it ended right here, right now.

"Good." She kissed him. "Let's go back to bed."

It wasn't any good, Hilary thought.

She sat down on the edge of her bed and stared off into space. She and Dev might have worked out their schedules over the past two weeks, but there was still the major problem that his business demanded early-morning hours and hers demanded nights. Their moments together had a stolen, frenzied quality to them, and with a two-and-a-half-hour drive between them, spontaneity was impossible.

Devlin kept saying things would get better and then added that it would be "in the fall," when his business slowed. Well, she knew better. Their basic lifestyles were too different, and there was enough distance between their homes to make the practicalities of a relationship tantalizing in theory and impractical in reality. Their relationship would not survive as a weekend one for very long.

Not with a man like Dev—*if* he even wanted a long-lasting relationship.

That was her biggest fear. The more time passed, the more positive she was that his interest in her was a form of rebellion. He never once said he cared for her, or talked about being together exclusively. Although, practically speaking, he didn't have the time to be with anyone else. Still, nothing had been said about seeing others, and nothing had been said that they wouldn't. Instead, he just chuckled over how wrong his grandmother was about them. If he said the word *unsuitable* one more time, she vowed she'd throw something at him.

It was time she stopped kidding herself and admitted the truth, Hilary thought. There had been no relationship until the moment, the literal moment, his grandmother had expressed disapproval of her. Then he'd turned from nasty boy to solicitous lover. He might have wanted her physically before that—men did have the urge to test every water they saw—but he hadn't wanted her emotionally. In fact he'd taken great pains to make that clear to her. The change in him had been abrupt—too abrupt. No matter how she tried to ignore it or tell herself differently, the truth had been there waiting until she was forced to turn it away.

Hilary glanced at the open suitcase on the bedroom chair. Closing her eyes, she shivered at the thought of two weeks on a cruise ship with Devlin. She couldn't back out now, even if she had the courage to do so. And she didn't. It really was a last-ditch effort with the grandparents, to try to generate something for them.

"Déjà vu," she muttered, knowing she'd talked

herself into several things with Devlin through the same argument. She knew her motives were selfish too. She wanted this time with him, and she didn't care where it left her emotionally in the aftermath. When they got home, though, she would have to break off with him. She couldn't go on the way she was, not and keep her emotional sanity.

Forcing herself to get up, she continued packing. The car to the cruise ship would be coming in just a few hours, and she still had several things to do before she left.

The telephone rang, and she answered it.

"It's me," Devlin said.

"Hello, me." She swallowed back the lump of despondency even as she forced herself to be casual.

He chuckled. She loved his chuckle.

"We need to make a slight change in plan," he said.

Marsh sat at the Flamingo bar, one of several on the *Princess Beatrice* luxury liner. He stared at the dwindling level of Scotch in his glass and proceeded to dwindle it some more.

"I see you're along for the ride too," Lettice said, sliding onto the bar stool next to him.

"You!" He turned sharply at the unexpected voice. He hadn't been expecting her, but somehow he wasn't surprised by her presence. "I had nothing better to do." He motioned to the bartender. "Gin and tonic for the lady."

"You remember."

He shrugged, then smiled. "It was easy to remember."

And it had been. Maybe it was time he stopped being so bullheaded and started admitting it. He'd done a lot of thinking about young girls and their freedoms sixty years ago. They hadn't had much. He'd even come to a reluctant realization or two. Besides, if he was stuck on the same boat with Lettice for two weeks, he might as well admit a certain amount of defeat. She was a familiar face in the crowd at least.

"They're not here, you know," she said.

"I know. I checked with the purser. They never got on board."

"Do you have the feeling we've been outwitted?"

"Without a doubt."

"I probably should tell you that I think our grandchildren are extremely suitable," she said, after taking a sip of her gin and tonic. "In fact I have always thought Dev would be lucky if he got Hilary."

"That's not what you said before," he reminded her.

"My grandson, idiot that he is, responds better in a defiant mode. I was attempting to get him to rebel in the right direction with what seemed like my disapproval of Hilary." Lettice smiled. "Instead he sicced you on me."

"He's not a bad kid," Marsh conceded.

"Except that he's related to me." She shrugged. "You can't have everything, Marsh."

He took a healthy swallow of the whiskey. It went down smooth and mellow. His indulgences were few and far between, for a person could get to like this too much. Just as a person could get to like the woman sitting next to him too much.

"I can't make up for what happened, Marsh," Lettice began.

He hushed her. "Shhh. It's the past."

"I'm in the mood to walk the treadmills in the gym," she said after a moment's silence. "Want to come with me? We can check our hearts afterward."

"Are you propositioning me?" he asked.

"Eventually."

"Then lead the way."

Dev had had plans, special plans.

"Screwed-up plans," he muttered, then cursed heartily. The day couldn't get any worse. His partner on the gambler dinner cruises to Atlantic City had fallen ill and couldn't make the run. Dev had had no choice but to do it. The ferry wasn't a small fishing boat. It required tougher licensing, which none of the rest of the crew had and which he did.

Now he was stuck with a boatload of hungry, screaming gamblers demanding the ride *and* their money back. Next time he took on a partner, he'd make damn sure they had a qualified backup captain. And that the backup had a backup. He was supposed to be a *silent* partner. This was the last time he'd ever do this—especially after taking out a charter that morning. He'd been up nearly twenty-four hours.

He had one bright spot. Hilary, when she'd heard of his predicament, had insisted on coming down and helping him. He didn't see what she could do, but he was grateful for her company. Maybe he could salvage something once they got to Atlantic City, he mused. Then he cursed again, remembering he had to take the gamblers back to Wildwood at one in the morning. Nothing was going right. He looked around for Hilary on the bridge. She wasn't there.

She was seasick again, he thought, feeling as if his worst nightmare were opening up before him.

"Take the wheel," he said to the other crew member. The man was cleared for open water.

After relinquishing the wheel, Dev scrambled down the gangway and headed for the saloons. People were gathered in little knots around the tables and bars, talking and chatting, waiting for dinner to be served. Hilary wasn't among them. He glanced at his watch as he passed through. The ferry would be docking in about an hour. The chef was cutting it close for dinner.

Hilary wasn't in the next saloon either, or on deck. He began to worry as he walked through the employee doors toward the stern, just in case she had wandered back there. But he knew the truth. She was in one of the ladies' rooms, clinging to a bowl for dear life. The night couldn't get any worse.

On the threshold of the galley he stopped dead and watched in amazement as Hilary, standing amid culinary chaos, calmly and expertly opened clams.

"You're not seasick," he said, dodging past a waiter to reach her.

She smiled briefly. "I would be if I had time."

"What are you doing in here?"

"Your chef's drunk. The guys tell me this isn't the first time. So I thought I'd help out." Her cool voice clearly showed her disdain for the man. When she turned to the waiters, though, she gave orders in a warm, gentle tone. "Marco, here's the last of the clams. Get the passengers in and started on their appetizers. Peter, turn those fillets while I start plating the food."

The men went to work, smiling gratefully at her. Dev didn't know how she was able to walk in and take over the way she had. Maybe the galley staff was too shorthanded to be anything but appreciative.

"You didn't have to do this," he said.

Her body stilled. She turned to him. "I owe you this, Devlin."

He frowned. Her words had an ominous ring to them, and her eyes looked almost . . . sad.

"Hilary," he began.

She smiled and shook her head. "We'll talk later. Now, go drive the boat."

He chuckled, as the others snorted in amusement. "Okay, I'll go 'drive' the boat."

There was no other woman in the world like her, he thought. All elegance and hidden passion, with new facets to discover every day. His little bump of uneasiness was unfounded. When he got her to Atlantic City, he'd make up for lost time. For a lot of lost time.

He turned back to the bridge, to "drive the boat."

Hilary slowly wiped down the last counter in the galley, trying to stretch the job out for as long as possible. She'd been hiding down here, ever since she'd discovered the cruise's chef drunk and the waiters running around like chickens with their heads cut off.

She shook her head in disgust as she thought of Devlin's partner who was cutting corners too sharply. One questionable chef to prepare a meal for fifty? No wonder the man got drunk. She really had to speak to Devlin before his investment went bankrupt. . . .

That was the problem, she admitted. She didn't want to speak to Devlin, because she'd have to speak about more than a business problem. Something she was *not* ready to do.

"Want to do a little gambling?"

She jumped at the sound of his voice and whipped around to face him. He was leaning against the doorway, hands in his jeans pockets, grinning knowingly at her.

"Did I scare you?" he asked, strolling into the galley.

"A little," she said stiffly, trying to keep an emotional distance.

"I can never thank you enough for your help." He put his arms around her. Though she tried to hold herself still and not respond, the feel of his body so close to hers was sending undeniable erotic signals through her. He added, "I even heard several of the passengers raving about the food when they left."

"Good," she said, trying to regain her control. "I was glad I could help."

"Want a job as a chef on a boat?"

She snorted. "No thanks."

"What's wrong?" he asked, straightening away from her.

She shrugged, then decided to get one topic started. She turned around to face him, but leaned back against the counter to keep her distance and her equilibrium. "I think your partner is making some bad judgments on these gambler cruises. You need more than one person for a kitchen staff if you're going to feed the kind of numbers you're feeding here. You especially don't need a chef whose reliability is questionable."

Devlin nodded. "So I've already seen. There's a

lot more going on here besides the problem in the galley. Changes will have to be made, if my money stays in."

"Oh." She was out of conversation. It was time. "Devlin, I've been doing a lot of thinking—"

"About us," he guessed, suddenly becoming wary.

She scrubbed at a nonexistent spot on the counter. "Yes."

"Look, if you're mad about what happened tonight, well, I'm sorry—"

"It's not tonight," she broke in, not looking at him. "It's . . . it's everything. We live so far away—"

"Move closer to me."

She gaped at him. "You move closer to me!"

"I have my business."

"And I have mine!"

"I know that. It's just that I couldn't move too far from the shore because of the hours. I was thinking that maybe you could turn over more of the business to Jane and Jeremy. . . . "

"Me? Me? You turn over more to Billy!"

"I've been thinking about it," he admitted.

That knocked some of the wind out of her sails. Hilary told herself to be rational, to control her temper. "It's not just that, Devlin. Our basic outlooks are completely different—"

"I know we've had some problems coordinating ourselves."

"And then we're only together for the sex."

"What else is there?" he asked, chuckling.

She straightened. "There's love."

He stared at her speechless.

She turned her back to him, knowing she'd opened her heart in a way she'd never meant to. "I know you don't feel the same way. I'm a form of rebellion to you, Devlin. I don't think you realize it, but I am."

"That's ridiculous!" he said.

"No, it isn't." She sighed and faced him again. "If you think about us for two minutes, you'd know it was true. You wanted absolutely nothing to do with me, until your grandmother decided we were 'unsuitable.'" She drew out the word sarcastically. "Then you couldn't get me into bed fast enough, and you've kept me there with every one of your grandmother's protests."

He gaped at her. "I've always tried to get you into bed! That had nothing to do with Grandmother."

"See? Just sex," she said triumphantly.

He glowered at her. "Hilary, I don't know what the hell is wrong, but you're spouting nonsense."

"I wish I were." She closed her eyes against a sharp thrust of pain, then opened them. She kept her gaze steady on his. "I tried to tell myself I was wrong, that it was silliness, insecurity, whatever. Devlin, you've rejected your family and what they stand for. You even named your boat what you did to prove it to the world—and to remind yourself to keep people at arm's length."

"Hilary—"

She went on, ignoring him. "You practically hated me at first, because you thought I was a hanger-on trying to break into all that. Your grandmother wanted us together then, remember? And then when she didn't, the next morning, *that very next morning*, you do a complete reversal."

"What about you?" he asked. "You weren't jumping for joy over me at first. One moment you didn't like me either. And then boom! You were all over me like peanut butter on bread."

"I was not!" she exclaimed, her cheeks heating. "I fell for you!"

"Did you ever think that maybe I did too?"

She shook her head, squeezing back the tears that threatened to spill. She was positive she was right. He would never see it, never admit it. That was just another form of his rebellion. "Not with your track record."

"You're practicing psychiatry without a license," he snapped.

"I'm telling you the truth!" she snapped back. "And when you're done rebelling, you'll realize this was all a mistake, apologize, and walk away. I can't wait for that. I can't!"

"Hi," Marco said, coming into the galley. Then he stopped, his eyes widening as he clearly caught on to the confrontation.

"I've had enough of this crap," Devlin said, and stalked out of the galley.

Hilary slumped against the counter.

"I'm sorry," Marco said. "I've interrupted."

Hilary blinked back her tears. "No. It was going in circles anyway."

And now, she thought, it wasn't going anywhere.

And he'd thought the day couldn't get any worse.

Dev swung the wheel viciously in his anger. The boat veered sharply toward the Wildwood docks. He corrected the steering and brought the boat into the berth without incident.

"Finish it up," he said to the nearest crew member. He made an effort not to snap at the man. It wouldn't be fair to take his mood out on an innocent bystander. Better to take it out on the walls . . . or the windows . . . or the equipment. . . .

Damn her, he thought as he left the still-intact bridge. He couldn't believe the ludicrous accusations she'd made in the galley. How could she even think those kinds of things about him? How could she say them?

He wouldn't ask, he decided. He had too much pride for that. His anger had built all the way home. She had hurt him in ways he'd never thought possible. He had thought—Clearly he'd been wrong about her. He had opened himself up to her, but she was just like all the rest. No, worse.

The stars were shining brightly as he stepped out onto the deck. He realized he hadn't seen Hilary since the incident in the galley. He had stayed on the bridge, and she had stayed who-knew-where. For all he knew, she could have left the ferry before it disembarked from Atlantic City.

She wouldn't have, he thought, looking frantically among the tired passengers gathering along the deck rails. It was too dark to make out faces, but logic told him she wouldn't have left her car behind in Wildwood. She would at least come back to get that.

He spotted her just coming up from below deck and heading toward the bow. He walked over and took her arm, pulling her away from the people.

"You're wrong," he said as soon as they were sheltered under the threshold to the forward saloon. "What can I do to convince you?"

She shook her head. "I'm not wrong. You know I'm not."

"I don't know a damn thing except this." He brought his mouth down on hers, his kiss almost savage in his desperation to show her the truth of his feelings. He hadn't meant to reveal to her how he felt, but nothing could keep it buried.

To his surprise her lips parted and she kissed him back, as desperately as he. Her hands gripped his windbreaker, her mouth like fire. He almost clung to her with hope.

"How can you say this is rebellion?" he murmured, kissing her hair.

She pressed her forehead into his shoulder. "Because that's all it is," she said, her voice breaking. "That's all I am to you. You just haven't realized it yet."

He tore himself away from her. "If that's what you want to believe, then go ahead and believe it, dammit!"

She swiped at her face. He realized she was crying, and he hardened his heart against the tears. Women always used tears to their advantage.

Straightening, she turned and left the boat. He watched her go, cursing her silly notions and her stubbornness.

He wasn't rebelling, he told himself. He wasn't.

But a little voice inside him rebelliously wondered if she was right.

"We're married!" Marsh exclaimed.

Hilary instantly burst into tears. Marsh chuckled at the thought that his granddaughter would pop her eyes when he told her he and Lettice were calling from Rio de Janeiro, on their sudden honeymoon. "I knew you'd be happy for us," he went on into the phone.

Hilary didn't answer, and something in his granddaughter's crying sparked an uneasiness in him. Puzzled, he said, "You *are* happy, aren't you, Hilary?"

The wails went up about ten decibels. All was definitely not well in Hilary Land.

Marsh immediately handed the receiver to his bride. "I don't know what the hell's wrong with her. You talk to her."

"Just like a man," Lettice said.

"You liked certain parts this morning," he reminded her.

"I take my pleasures where I can get them."

He harrumphed a reply, then listened as Lettice talked soothingly to his granddaughter, calming her and then probing. All he could discern from the one-sided conversation was that something had happened with Devlin.

"They broke up," Lettice said when she finally hung up.

"Broke up?" Marsh repeated. "Why would they break up?"

"Because Hilary's decided she's Dev's latest form of rebellion."

"Dammit, woman!" Marsh roared. "You and your meddling did this!"

Lettice eyed her new husband for a long moment, then said, "Stop bellowing like a wounded bull. My grandson is more wary than a prairie dog poking his head out at buffalo mating time. Somebody had to light a fire under his tail. Hilary unfortunately took it all the wrong way and now can't see past her nose on this. I'll call Devlin."

As she dialed, Lettice scrambled for solutions to this new turn of events. One thing she hadn't expected was Hilary's perception and her reaction to it. She supposed she could understand the girl's hurt—but what did it matter how Devlin got started, just as long as he did? The transcontinental connection took a few minutes, but finally her grandson was on the other line.

"Marsh and I got married two days ago," she announced, beginning the conversation with a bang.

"Congratulations." Devlin's voice was flat and devoid of emotion.

"You could fake your cheerfulness a little better than that," she said.

His exasperated intake of breath was audible over the line. "I am happy for you, and tell Marsh I said he's a fool. Okay?"

"That's better. Now, what are you going to do about Hilary?"

"Who told you? Her?" He didn't wait for an answer. "What the hell am I supposed to do?"

"Have you talked to her?"

"Why bother? She's convinced I'm rebelling—"

"Well, of course you were!" Lettice snapped in her own exasperation. "Somebody had to push a few buttons just to get you over the edge."

"You . . . Damn you, Grandmother!"

"Oh, stop fussing. You were already on the precipice, silly boy. I leave you two alone for five minutes and you make a disaster of everything."

"Me!"

"Yes, you. Well, you'll just have to fix it."

"And how do you propose I do that?"

"Stop being an ass. All you have to do is prove she's wrong about how you feel."

"*I don't have to prove a damn thing!*" Devlin roared.

"I'm not going to have any ears left at this rate," Lettice muttered, holding the receiver far away. A loud click came over the wire, then the dial tone. Her grandson had hung up on her.

"Foolish boy," she murmured, replacing the receiver. No one hung up on her and got away with it.

"How are you going to fix this one?" Marsh asked.

"I'm not," she said righteously. "I never meddle."

Marsh burst into laughter.

"I don't see why I have to go," Hilary said, crossing her arms over her chest. "And I don't see why I have to wear this!"

"You have to go because a family member is sponsoring the event, and you *will* do it for Lettice's sake," Marsh said, steering the car into the temporary parking lot along the river.

"And you're wearing that dress," Lettice added, "because it's appropriate. Now, uncross your arms before you muss the pleats."

Hilary reluctantly uncrossed her arms and smoothed out the stiffened silk of her gown. The long skirt was black and hugged her legs, just as the strapless top hugged her torso. A wide band of pleated white satin wrapped around her waist. The dress was beautiful, and Lettice was right about it being appropriate, but she felt half-naked with her shoulders exposed.

When they emerged from the car, Hilary took a deep breath, then had to resist the urge to yank up her bodice. It wouldn't go anywhere anyway. There wasn't enough material. At least she wouldn't be cold as the evening grew longer. This first weekend in September was still hot enough for it to feel like the middle of summer rather than the end. Someone had had a good idea in holding the charity ball on the docks of Penn's Landing in Philadelphia.

Why had she come to this thing? she asked herself. Because it was Devlin's charity ball. Because she was proud of what he was doing. And because she wanted to see him again. Just see him. With their families connected now, she couldn't avoid a meeting forever. She'd told herself she had to prove she could see him and still stay numb. Now, however, it didn't seem like such a good idea.

"Are you going to stand there, or does your grandfather have to carry you?" Lettice asked.

"I'd get ten hernias," Marsh said.

"Thanks," Hilary muttered.

Lettice looped her arm through Hilary's. "Come on. He's not here anyway."

Hilary gaped as the older woman pulled her forward. "He isn't?" She immediately shrugged to show her unconcern. "That's his business."

"So he said. He's back in hibernation." Lettice looked around at the formally dressed crowd. "Who cares as long as he put the money up? We've got a good crowd. Now, let's take 'em for everything they've got."

Hilary chuckled. Knowing Devlin wouldn't be there made her relax a little. But once they entered the cordoned-off area, her grandparents disappeared to talk with old friends. Although she nodded and said hello to people she knew, she felt like a stranger, accidentally misplaced among her clients. Normally she was on the other end, and she watched, with envy, the waiters circulating with their trays. She didn't belong here, and in truth she'd never wanted to. What had been a source of bitterness for her grandfather, a source of eternal hope and frustration for her parents, was only a source of income for her. She felt more aligned to Devlin than to whatever the past had held for her family.

She also found herself watching for one particular man. Her stomach dropped when she thought she spotted him, but she recognized Catherine Wagner-Kitteridge at his side and realized she was looking at Miles, Devlin's twin. Curious, she studied Miles's face. While he looked like his brother at first glance, there were many faint differences between them. Miles's nose was a little smaller, the lines of his face were less prominent, his skin color was lighter, his haircut was more precise. He held himself differently too. In fact he wasn't a bit like Devlin, she thought.

"Stop it!" she muttered, snatching a long-stemmed champagne glass off the tray of a passing waiter. She took a sip, then wrinkled her nose and stared down at the glass.

It was the cheap stuff. Very cheap stuff.

She smiled, remembering another time with the cheap stuff. Then she forced the memory away and told herself for the millionth time that it never would have worked with Devlin. And just as she had over the past weeks without him, she wished there was some way she could have been proven wrong. Summer was supposed to be all brilliant sunshine and heat, but it would never be that way for her again.

She wandered around for a little while before finding a quiet spot by the quay, stepping carefully so that her heels wouldn't catch in between the planks. The tall ships, their masts standing proud, were an elegant backdrop to the elegant party. Up close they were even more beautiful, and she understood why these sailing vessels graced the sea rather than rode it.

Something odd caught her eye a little farther along the dock, and she got up and walked over slowly. As she neared it, her heart thumped painfully. There, among the exquisite ships, was a squat boat with a wide center fly bridge. The name on the stern was *For the Love of Hilary*.

She stared at it in shock, then took a large gulp of champagne. It went down like an octane fire. He had changed the name of his boat. The words rang through her head like a litany.

"You keep drinking that stuff and we'll have to have your stomach pumped."

She spun around to find Devlin behind her. He was dressed for the occasion in a white dinner jacket and he looked terrific. But his darkened skin and pronounced crow's feet proved he was no stodgy businessman. She valiantly resisted the urge to throw herself at him.

"You ordered it, didn't you?" she said, surprised at the calmness of her voice.

He grinned. "I don't think anyone's noticed the difference except you."

She smiled. "You're not supposed to be here."

"Who says?"

"Your grandmother."

"She lies."

"Yes, I know."

They were silent for a long moment, neither moving.

"I'm sorry if you were hurt," he said finally, his gaze searching hers. "But, Hilary, what the hell does it matter how something starts? What matters is how it ends. I like who I am and what I do, and I'm not going to change. I love who you are and what you do, and I don't want you to change. But I don't want to wait sixty years, like our grandparents, before coming to our senses."

"Neither do I." She practically flew into his arms, the champagne glass spilling unnoticed to the planks as they embraced. The kiss was fierce and gentle with promise, all at the same time.

She tore her lips from his and spread kisses on his cheeks and jaw and forehead, all the while chanting, "I love you, I love you."

He nuzzled her throat. "I love you, Hilary. I'll spend a lifetime making it up to you."

"You're damn straight on that," she murmured.

He laughed, then grew serious. "Do you mean it?"

"Yes," she said, positive. By changing the name of his boat, he had given her an incredible sign of his feelings and commitment to her. If he could do that, then so could she.

"Let's go home," he said. "You can show me how that dress stays up."

"Trick photography."

"As long as the rest of you is real."

"It is."

"Then let's go home."

Epilogue

"This is the last time you get me into one of these damn tuxes," Dev said as he led his new bride onto the dance floor.

"Quit complaining," Hilary said, wrapping her gown's ivory-satin train around her arm. "Ready."

He waltzed her around for the traditional newlywed dance. "I told you not to let Grandmother go hog-wild over the wedding plans."

"It made her happy. Now, stop fussing."

"I'm happy when I'm fussing," he said, then grinned at her. "But I'll be happier when we're naked and on the honeymoon. Can we do that now?"

"No." She smiled. "Anticipation is everything."

He leaned forward and whispered, "Everything is me inside you."

She sighed. "You'll never change. Thank goodness."

He pulled her closer, deeply content. He had gone down in flames before love, and he couldn't find anything more satisfying than loving Hilary.

She had taught him to live with himself again—even to like himself. She had also taught him to stop punishing everyone around him. He still liked the freedom he'd discovered, but he could accept his past and his family again—although he was beginning to have his doubts about his grandmother.

Hell, he thought. Lettice was happy, Hilary was happy, and in a few hours, when he was naked and on his honeymoon, he'd be happy too.

"I haven't given you my wedding gift yet," Hilary whispered.

He lifted his head. "I thought I got that last night."

"Basic sustenance." She grew serious. "Jane and Jeremy are taking over the business here. I'm going to open a branch store and catering business. In Wildwood."

He stared at her in astonishment. "But I thought we were going to move halfway between the businesses."

"It would never have worked."

"We've got to do something about your optimism," he said.

She laughed. "I believe I just did. The business here is doing well, and Jane and Jeremy have the know-how and the contacts. I think the branch will be adventurous—"

"And I thought you were doing it for love."

"And fun."

He stopped dancing and pulled her to him, kissing her soundly. Everyone at the reception applauded.

"I love you," he said, when he finally raised his head.

She smiled through her tears. "Not as much as I love you."

"We could debate that forever."

"I intend to."

He chuckled, and twirled her around the dance floor.

After the requisite dance, they joined his family. Lettice and Marsh were surrounded by her grandchildren. Dev tolerated the kidding from his relatives and his grandmother's exceptionally smug expression. He acknowledged they weren't a bad bunch as a family. A little misguided as to the finer things in life, but not bad.

"Look at her," he said, pointing to Lettice. "She thinks she played matchmaker again."

"I did," Lettice said.

Everyone burst into laughter, except for Marsh, who looked completely bewildered.

"No, you didn't," Ellen Kitteridge-Carlini said. "We arranged *you* this time."

"That's right," said Anne Kitteridge-Farraday, laughing gleefully. "Catherine called a family meeting after your last stunt."

"We gave you the idea of Hilary for Dev," Susan Kitteridge-St. Jacques added.

"Dev and Hilary agreed to go along with the arrangement to get you and Marsh together," Susan's brother, Rick, said, grinning at his grandmother.

"And you fell for it!" Miles said, laughing.

"We're really sorry you were the victim," Dev said to Marsh.

Marsh shrugged. "She grows on you after a while."

"Are you all done being proud of yourselves?" Lettice asked. Everyone laughed more loudly until she added, "I would like to remind you that we are at Devlin and Hilary's wedding."

"A technicality," Dev said.

"A major coup," Lettice corrected him, "considering how tough a nut you were to crack. That's why I left you for last. For a long time I thought Hilary was perfect for you . . . and for a long time I've wanted to make things up with Marsh." She smiled at her husband, then the smile became sly as she turned back to her grandchildren. "You don't honestly think James's grandmother pulled Marsh's name out from thin air, do you? I've been expecting you all to take revenge for some time. Lavinia was primed for months."

Everyone gaped at her.

"And it certainly took you long enough!" she added in clear disgust. "I thought you'd never figure it out!"

Miles's wife, Catherine, was the first to find her voice. "She's trying to make herself look good, now that it's over."

"Forget it, *chère*," Susan's husband, Remy, said.

"No way," Ellen's husband, Joe, and Anne's husband, James, said together.

Rick's wife, Jill, just shook her head.

"I have always 'helped' you find love and happiness, because I had lost mine," Lettice said, patting Marsh's hand. "I wasn't brave enough to keep it. This does not take away from your grandfather or Marsh's wife. They were wonderful people and we loved them. But you almost never get a second chance in a lifetime. Thanks to your being led down the garden path—and you all went the right way—I've now got mine."

Everyone was silent for a long minute, until Dev

finally said, "Right, and next you'll have a bridge to sell me."

"There is this one . . ." Lettice began.

The family started laughing.

"At least she's done," someone said.

"There's always the great-grandchildren," Lettice reminded them.

"*No!*"

Lettice smiled.

THE EDITOR'S CORNER

With the six marvelous **LOVESWEPT**s coming your way next month, it certainly will be the season to be jolly. Reading the best romances from the finest authors—what better way to enter into the holiday spirit?

Leading our fabulous lineup is the ever-popular Fayrene Preston with **SATAN'S ANGEL,** LOVESWEPT #510. Nicholas Santini awakes after a car crash and thinks he's died and gone to heaven—why else would a beautiful angel be at his side? But Angel Smith is a flesh-and-blood woman who makes him burn with a desire that lets him know he's very much alive. Angel's determined to work a miracle on this magnificent man, to drive away the pain—and the peril—that torments him. A truly wonderful story, written with sizzling sensuality and poignant emotions—one of Fayrene's best!

How appropriate that Gail Douglas's newest LOVESWEPT is titled **AFTER HOURS,** #511, for that's when things heat up between Casey McIntyre and Alex McLean. Alex puts his business—and heart—on the line when he works *very* closely with Casey to save his newspaper. He's been betrayed before, but Casey inspires trust . . . and brings him to a fever pitch of sensual excitement. She never takes orders from anyone, yet she can't seem to deny Alex's passionate demands. A terrific book, from start to finish.

Sandra Chastain weaves her magical touch in **THE-JUDGE AND THE GYPSY,** LOVESWEPT #512. When Judge Rasch Webber unknowingly shatters her father's dream, Savannah Ramey vows a Gypsy's revenge: She would tantalize him beyond reason, awakening longings he's denied, then steal what he most loves. She couldn't know she'd be entangled in a web of desire, drawn to the velvet caress of Rasch's voice and the ecstatic fulfillment in his arms. You'll be thoroughly enchanted with this story of forbidden love.

The combination of love and laughter makes **MIDNIGHT KISS** by Marcia Evanick, LOVESWEPT #513, completely irresistible. To Autumn O'Neil, Thane Clayborne is a sexy stick-in-the-mud, and she delights in making him lose control. True, running a little wild is not Thane's style, but Autumn's seductive beauty tempts him to let go. Still, she's afraid that the man who bravely sacrificed a dream for another's happiness could never care for a woman who ran scared when it counted most. Another winner from Marcia Evanick!

With his tight jeans, biker boots, and heartbreak-blue eyes, Michael Hayward is a **TEMPTATION FROM THE PAST**, LOVESWEPT #514, by Cindy Gerard. January Stewart has never seen a sexier man, but she knows he's more trouble that she can handle. Intrigued by the dedicated lawyer, Michael wants to thaw January's cool demeanor and light her fire. Is he the one who would break down her defenses and cast away her secret pain? Your heart will be stirred by this touching story.

A fitting final course is **JUST DESSERTS** by Theresa Gladden, LOVESWEPT #515. Caitlin MacKenzie has had it with being teased by her new housemate, Drew Daniels, and she retaliates with a cream pie in his face! Pleased that serious Caitie has a sense of humor to match her lovely self, Drew begins an ardent pursuit. She would fit so perfectly in the future he's mapped out, but Catie has dreams of her own, dreams that could cost her what she has grown to treasure. A sweet and sexy romance—what more could anybody want?

FANFARE presents four truly spectacular books this month! Don't miss bestselling Amanda Quick's **RENDEZVOUS**. From London's most exclusive club to an imposing country manor, comes this provocative tale about a free-thinking beauty, a reckless charmer, and a love that defied all logic. **MIRACLE**, by beloved LOVESWEPT author Deborah Smith, is the unforgettable contemporary romance of passion and the collision of worlds, where a man and a woman who couldn't have been more different learn that love may be improbable, but never impossible.

Immensely talented Rosalind Laker delivers the exquisite historical **CIRCLE OF PEARLS**. In England during the days of plague and fire, Julia Pallister's greatest test comes from an unexpected quarter—the man she calls enemy, a man who will stop at nothing to win her heart. And in **FOREVER,** by critically acclaimed Theresa Weir, we witness the true power of love. Sammy Thoreau had been pronounced a lost cause, but from the moment Dr. Rachel Collins lays eyes on him, she knows she would do anything to help the bad-boy journalist learn to live again.

Happy reading!

With every good wish for a holiday filled with the best things in life,

Nita Taublib

Nita Taublib
Associate Publisher/LOVESWEPT
Publishing Associate/FANFARE

FANFARE

Now On Sale

MIRACLE

☐ (29107-6) $4.50/5.50 in Canada
by Deborah Smith

author of THE BELOVED WOMAN

A man and a woman who couldn't have been more different -- all it took to bring them together was a MIRACLE. "Ever witty, a sparkling talent with a unique voice." -- Rendezvous

CIRCLE OF PEARLS

☐ (29423-7) $5.99/6.99 in Canada
by Rosalind Laker

author of TO DANCE WITH KINGS

Why is Julia Pallister so drawn to the man she is sure she despises, the enemy her Royalist stepfather would have her marry? "A book to sit back and enjoy like a sumptuous feast." -- Rave Reviews

FOREVER

☐ (29380-X) $4.50/5.50 in Canada
by Theresa Weir

author of AMAZON LILY

They said he was a lost cause, but they didn't know what love could do. "[A] hauntingly beautiful and passionate love story." -- Rendezvous

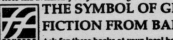

"Funny and heartrending . . . wonderful characters . . . I laughed out loud and couldn't stop reading. A splendid romance!" -- *Susan Elizabeth Phillips*, <u>New York Times</u> *bestselling author of FANCY PANTS and HOT SHOT*

Miracle

by

Deborah Smith

An unforgettable story of love and the collision of two worlds. From a shanty in the Georgia hills to a television studio in L.A., from the heat and dust of Africa to glittering Paris nights -- with warm, humorous, passionate characters, MIRACLE weaves a spell in which love may be improbable but never impossible.